Pioneer Legacy

Based on the life of
Elizabeth Jones Fox

Pioneer Legacy

Written by

Lynne Thompson

Publisher's Note

The phrases in parenthesis and italics refer to the song tracks on the CD entitled: *Pioneer Legacy* with music by David Thompson featuring vocalist Katie Thompson.

Cover design and illustrations by Bryan Ferre.

Published by:
ASAP Productions

Contact and Order information:
ASAP Productions
1722 S 200 E
Orem, UT 84058
Email: dthomp@transedge.com

ISBN: 1-57636-142-X

Dedicated to

My husband David and our children who
have provided me with great life
experiences, love, and support.

Acknowledgements

Thanks to the family historians, Jay Burrup and Faye Burrows and to all of the descendants of Elizabeth and George Fox who shared their historical information and preserved her life history.

Thanks also to my dear husband, David, who composed the beautiful music for Pioneer Legacy. He never doubted that I could actually write a book about Elizabeth. He read and reread and prodded me on. I played the Pioneer Legacy CD over and over as I typed. It inspired me and helped me keep the vision of the work.

The collaborative process has amazing power. Many people contributed their time, skills and talents.

To Gayann DeMordaunt, David Squires and Mary Jo Tanner who read the manuscript and made hundreds of margin notes and suggestions, I can't thank you enough. Your knowledge of writing skills and detailed input were invaluable.

Thanks to all of the people who read the first edition and contributed their ideas: Caroline Judd, Bruce McMaster, Bonnie Pence, Lulie Blackham, Adonna Patch, Nancy Nordlund, Deborah Peterson, Sarah Thompson, Lee Friske, Marla Wilcock, Martha Hagett, Jill Hughes, Neal Tanner and Shanna Nerdin. Also to my Grandson, Paul D. Judd, who helped with the fine-tuning.

A special thanks to Joe Belnap and Brian Carter who advised and guided in the publishing process.

Preface

This book is unique because it is based on a true story and it can be accompanied by the Pioneer Legacy Soundtrack. The story is inspiring with or without music. But if you choose to read it with music, this is how it works: places are marked throughout the book where the music fits the theme of the story. For example, when they are on the ship, the Pioneer Legacy Theme is played. The seagulls call in the background with Celtic melodies and powerful lyrics, thus you feel the spirit of the emigrants on the ship as you read about them. It is an unusual experience. It makes Elizabeth's story live.

I read many accounts of brave women who endured and sacrificed on the trek to Zion, but when I read about the life of Elizabeth Jones Fox, I knew her story needed to be told. From the first day on the *S.S. Curling* to the last day of the trek, her life was abundant in trials laced with miracles: the miracle of birth—the first day of sailing, the miracle of angels' protection, the miracle in the wilderness. It is truly a story of miracles.

Her trials, like many of the pioneers, are beyond our comprehension. But, we can relate. We can draw on the strength of their stories and enhance our lives.

My inspiration came twenty-five years ago, when I saw a sculpture of a pioneer woman on her knees, lifting her baby toward heaven. Her face was serene, although there were tears on her cheeks. I felt peace when I looked at her eyes. I stood in awe and wept. During my tour of the art show I found myself returning again and again to that sculpture, always feeling the same impact. Elizabeth's story impresses me in the same way. It reminds me of the need to rely on the Savior in our trials. I never tire of it, whether listening to the CD, working with the production or reading the book. Elizabeth's story is inspiring and faith promoting.

People have wanted to know how much of the story is true. The significant events in her life have been reconstructed with artistic license. She gave birth to a baby boy the first day of sailing to America. The angels surrounded the *S.S. Curling* during a storm. She contracted a breast infection (milk fever) and her baby died of starvation. She did get lost on the plains and how she crossed the river is still unknown. She did get care at Fort Bridger and was found in the manner described. The historical characters in the book are in their true settings and some have the same characteristics or personality traits as described in the book. For example, Israel Barlow was assigned to accompany the emigrants on the *S.S. Curling*, Milo Andrus was the wagon train leader, his wife loved music. In fact it was her piano that made it part way and had to be buried and retrieved later. However, she didn't write the lyrics to *Remember Him*. You get the idea. It is a story of mystery and miracles, one that strengthens resolve and increases faith.

The book and the Pageant, *Pioneer Legacy* are based on the life of Elizabeth Jones Fox. The music produced especially for *Pioneer Legacy* has a universal message: Come unto Christ and the importance of loving relationships.

Sometimes I felt as if Elizabeth were sitting beside me as I typed the manuscript. I have come to know her as I've explored the joys and sorrows in her life. I look forward to meeting her someday.

As my husband and I have discussed the process of creating this tribute to Elizabeth, and to all pioneers, we are convinced that we were merely the vessels through which it came. We know our skills were enhanced, and inspiration was sometimes a daily experience giving heed to the question of how much came from us or through us. We're not sure, but we love her story and feel privileged to tell it.

Table of Contents

Fox Family Tree

William Jones   Maria Reed   Richard Fox   Mary Selman

Elizabeth Jones 1823   George Selman Fox 1819

Elizabeth Mary Fox 1842

Thomas James Fox 1845

Desdemona Fox 1847

George Fox 1850

Charlotte Fox 1852

Sanders Curling Fox 1855

David Fox 1856

Heber John Fox 1859

Sarah Jane Fox 1861

Franklin Richard Fox 1864

Author's Note

This book has been enjoyed by many, in and of itself however, the reading experience is heightened if it is accompanied by the Pioneer Legacy Soundtrack. Places are marked in the book where the music fits the story. It is amazingly powerful and touches every emotion making the story come alive.

*References to Pioneer Legacy CD soundtracks are indicated by
The name of the song and selection number in italics.*

Chapter One

The Birth

Pioneer Legacy Theme (1) *followed by* **Hopes and Dreams (2)**

Gray skies blanketed Liverpool on this brisk April morning. *(Pioneer Legacy Theme–1)* Screaming seagulls seemed to call farewell as they swooped in search of food from the harbor where ships of every size and design were anchored. The passengers of the *S.S. Curling* leaned over the side rails waving last goodbyes. Tearful friends stood on the shore daubing their eyes and waving their white handkerchiefs in a final farewell. A tugboat began its relentless tow down the Mersey River and past Rock Lighthouse. With mixed emotions the emigrants watched the shoreline of their beloved England shrink and slowly disappear. Some cried, some laughed, some whispered, some sang, and some peeled the oranges that loved ones had thrown from shore as a parting gift. Faces turned toward the sea with hopes for a new life in a new land where the miracles of the gospel awaited them. They had no awareness of the different kind of miracle unfolding for the Fox family below deck.

"Oh, no, here it comes again. It's coming, it's coming. Oh, oh, ooooh." Elizabeth's short breaths escaped as her sweat-streaked face grimaced. She tossed and turned on the hard bunk, "I can't bear this any longer!" She closed her eyes tightly trying to subdue the pain.

"Where is George?" she moaned. "Charlotte?" She squeezed her sister-in-law's hand as if that would somehow bring relief.

"Ah, Betsy," soothed Charlotte as she pressed a damp rag to her brow. "It won't be long now and you'll have another sweet babe in your arms. George will be here soon enough."

Elizabeth didn't hear the last words as a tremendous pressure forced her to push with all her strength. She sat up slightly with legs spread wide, not aware of the hustle about her. In a time-honored way women hung quilts from the surrounding bunks creating a shelter of privacy for the moment of birth.

The round-faced midwife bent over her, one hand on her hip and the other on the moving mound. She nodded her head with an all-knowing expression and pressed firmly. Her graying hair was in a knot atop her head and a stained white apron with deep pockets covered her broad belly.

"There, there now, Mum. It's goin' t' be a fine delivery. That it 'tis." Turning to Charlotte she clucked, "Brave soul she is, and quite a beauty too this bein' her sixth child and all. Don't know 'ow these young ones does it, I don't."

Around this unfolding drama, one could see a sense of order and social propriety. Married couples occupied the central section of hundreds of bunks creating a barrier between the single women who occupied the stern and the single men who held claim to the section in the bow. Wicker baskets, wooden trunks, woven satchels, and bails of strapped clothing crammed every available nook and cranny in the hold. The ever-present smell of fish and mildew seemed to almost disappear with time as noses adjusted to the unpleasant odor.

The children were in a world of their own as they played hide-and-go-seek and hunt-the-slipper. A cluster of boys in short trousers and woolen hats knelt in the corner where their best shooting marbles clashed for supremacy. Thomas Fox, Elizabeth and George's oldest son, and his newly found friends mimicked the sailors. In the deepest voices they could muster the swaggering lads sang out, "Haul, haul away, haul away, Joe." Mothers tried in vain to quiet them but a sense of adventure filled the air, not to be dampened by any "shhhh." Their songs faded when the unfamiliar pitch and roll of the ship caught up with their inexperienced sea legs. Soon their swimming heads and upset stomachs prompted a hurried trip to the deck for relief.

Elder Barlow, the senior Church official of the group, kept pace with George who listened intently for the first faint cries of a newborn. They made an odd-looking pair pacing about the deck. George, handsome and lean, with blue eyes and short brown hair stood a full head above the round-faced, portly Elder Barlow.

"Slow and easy does it, George," Elder Barlow puffed, challenged by the brisk, lengthy strides. "It's not like this is the first or last to enter this world."

Mary, the oldest daughter, had begged to stay and watch the birth, and her Father had considered it, but at last thought it best for her to help him keep the other two in line. Desdemona, their youngest daughter, flitted about the ship from one end to the other, and he feared she could flit overboard at any given moment.

"Mary, you stay right close to her." George gave unnecessary instructions for Mary began caring for her little sister when she was six years old. Thomas was usually helpful but his incessant teasing of Desdemona brought her to the brink of tears. Only Mary's patience kept the peace.

"Go play with your friends. I'll let you know when your new little sister comes."

"Ain't going to be a girl! We need another man in the Fox family." With a look of mocked disgust, he ran off to join the marble game.

Charlotte stroked Elizabeth's long chestnut hair that draped across her thin shoulders and spread across the pillow.

"Ah, I hope this little one has your beautiful green eyes!" Charlotte noted the contractions were coming closer and longer now, exceeding the lapse of time between them. Elizabeth gasped for breath.

"Breathe, and relax," Charlotte suggested as she took her hand again.

"One more. Push 'arder this time, mum," came the wise voice of experience. Being firm and direct helped steady her patients. She held on to the bedpost for a surer footing as the ship pitched to the left.

Elizabeth grabbed the sides of the bunk to keep from rolling onto the floor. She was getting accustomed to the pitch and roll, first up in the front, then up in the back, then over to the left, and over to the right. It was no wonder that everyone was sick and the smell of vomit met her nostrils. She had long ago lost her stomach's contents. It seemed a minor inconvenience.

Harder, how do you push harder? Her face contorted and her eyes squeezed shut once again as she pushed with every muscle locked into the effort. An involuntary moan escaped her.

I can do this. I really can do this. Push! Her thoughts drove her body past its limit. Just when she thought she would burst like a dropped melon, it was over. The welcome release of life to life. An inexplicable joy washed over her. A feeling that she had felt five times before. Ever the same. A sense of oneness with nature, of communion with God, of perfect peace. *(Hopes and Dreams–2)*

"It's a boy, Betsy," Charlotte said with quiet reverence. "A new baby boy and a wee one at that."

"A boy! Are you sure?" She struggled to raise herself up on her elbows but she collapsed as the spinning room engulfed her.

"Sure 'tis I can be," chuckled the midwife. "He even cries like a boy. Listen to that bellow." Tiny legs and arms swam in the warm, salty air.

"Is he of good health? Does he look all right? Does he have all his fingers and toes?" All of her worries from the past nine months were wrapped up in these three questions.

"You'll see soon enough." The midwife wrapped the baby in a thin, plaid blanket and placed him in his mother's arms.

Suddenly George burst into the sanctuary of quilts. "I heard! Are you all right?" As he dropped to one knee he took her hands into his and kissed her on the cheek.

"Ah, Betsy, a boy! Isn't it wonderful? It's a boy!" George was beside himself. He poked his head out of the quilted interior and yelled, "it's a boy! A healthy baby boy!" Cheers could be heard across the deck. Congratulations from the chaps in the hold peppered in.

"George, the baby's all right. What about you?"

"Congratulations to you, George."

"Righto! George, you're a lucky man, you are."

How precious new life is, Elizabeth reflected. *And just look at George, so proud and happy. I love you, George, I surely do.*

"He will be a good man of God, he will." George made a declaration of faith as Elizabeth gave the baby to his Father.

"Ahhhhh, he is beautiful," she said reverently. "He looks just like little Georgie did, doesn't he? Those big eyes and such a wee nose, he does look just like him."

Not listening, George stared intently into his baby's face waiting for another glimpse of open eyes. Elizabeth blinked back the tears as she remembered her little Georgie and baby Charlotte.

I'll rock this wee one as I did all my babes. She closed her eyes. *We brought the rocking chair and...*

She shuddered as her thoughts wandered through those last dark days just over a year ago. She could still hear her children gasping for breath between spells of coughing. Then the prickly looking rash appeared in warm places under their arms and on their stomachs. Fevers rose and their appetites disappeared as their small bodies were covered with measles. After days and nights of rocking and singing, cuddling and praying, Georgie, age three, and Charlotte, eighteen months, passed on within hours of each other. They were laid to rest in one tiny coffin.

I know they're looking down at their new baby brother... waiting for me to rock him.

Her thoughts were interrupted with the creaking of the ship. *Just like the creaking of the rocking chair...*

Elizabeth returned to the midwife's broad, toothy smile.

"There you be, mum, you're as good as new, y' are." The portly midwife stood, her back still bent from her work, and tucked the patterned quilt under Elizabeth's tiny feet with an eye of appreciation. Quilting was Elizabeth's favorite pastime and her handiwork was much admired. "Small feet for a strong soul," she muttered. "See that she rests, George. Her labor's been a hard 'un and she'll be needin' some sleep, I should think." She shuffled down the aisle. "I'll peep in on her after supper. I'm feelin' a bit queasy myself, I am. Might lie down a bit."

Elizabeth was wide-awake. She couldn't think of sleep, only her precious baby. *How beautiful he is,* she thought. *So tiny and so sweet.*

Closing her eyes she gave thanks silently for the miracle of life given on this first day of sailing.

"I'll go tell the children after I get one more peek." Charlotte peered at the baby. "A lovely baby, Betsy. Will you be naming him William after your Father?"

Elizabeth couldn't take her eyes from her tiny miracle. "Don't you just love his toes? The best part of a new baby is their teensy toes, and, of course their long fingers, just right for playing the concertina like his Father," Elizabeth mused, not hearing the query.

"He will grow up to be just like you, George, he will—strong, with quality looks and intelligence. And," she paused, "he will live in Zion." She slipped her finger into the tiny hand and the baby's fingers gently curled around hers.

She gazed beyond her baby as she recalled the stories of the Great Salt Lake. A gleaming white house came into view. She walked down the narrow cobblestone path that curved through rose bushes covered with red and pink blossoms. She reached for a rose and touched the velvet petals.

I shall pick one for you, my baby and put it on your cradle. She sighed as the faint grip loosened on her finger and once again his little face became real.

I shall take care of you, she promised. *We love you so much.* She kissed his soft head. *Your Father will teach you a trade and*

*I shall teach you about Jesus and...*her thoughts trailed as she became drowsy.

George had made a fair living as a gas tube maker selling his original lamps. However, he lost most of his customers when he joined the "crazy" Mormons. For eight long years they saved every farthing to meet the call to gather to Zion. When it came time to leave, their passage of fifteen pounds per person received supplemental funds from the Perpetual Emigration Fund, an ongoing assistance program for emigrants. Elder Barlow told them they could repay it from their labors after they reached Salt Lake.

"What shall we name him?" George asked.

"Sanders Curling."

George jerked with surprise as his eyes searched hers. He hadn't expected an answer, but a discussion.

"After a ship?"

"Well, not just a ship. I want to honor the fine captain and his ship."

Sanders Curling, of Thomaston, Maine, was part owner and captain of the *S.S. Curling*, an American Yankee square rigger. In England, he had the reputation of being a kind and devoted seaman. As they were boarding, Elizabeth overheard the Captain tell his steward to keep an eye on her situation and inform him when her time came. She appreciated his concern.

"Well, George, do you have a tongue? What do you think?"

"My Betsy, you never cease to amaze me! Sanders Curling it will be, or, do you think he should be Sanders Curling Fox?" he teased. He leaned over the bed and kissed her.

"And George, couldn't we bless him at the Sunday meeting?"

"Are you sure that's not too soon? That's only three days from now, Betsy, and he's so small and you..."

"George, I want him blessed at the next Sunday meeting," she declared. If she could have stood up she would have stamped her petite foot on the wooden planked floor. "Please ask Elder Barlow." She softened her approach with a half smile and a twinkle in her eye. "Please?"

"All right, I'll ask him this evening."

"I can't wait for the children to see the baby." She held her baby on her shoulder, gently patting his back and rubbing her cheek against his soft head.

"Sounds like they'll be here soon." George looked toward the doorway as footsteps clattered on the wooden stairs. Desdemona, brown braids bouncing and freckled face beaming, ducked under the steward's arms, around some ladies' long skirts, down the stairs and smack into the midwife who was leaning over straightening her blankets. Knocked headlong into her bunk, the midwife stood up, untwisted her apron and smoothed her gray hair into place.

"What y' runnin' laik a wild hare knockin' people over?"

"Oh, sorry." Desdemona stumbled backwards a few steps, curtsied politely and stammered, "so sorry, goin' to see my baby brother."

"Git off with ya then!" The midwife chuckled and pointed down the aisle.

Desdemona was still panting as she leaned over the bunk as far as her eight-year-old body could stretch.

"Oh, my," she brushed a wisp of hair from her eyes, "I'm your big sister, I am." Her green eyes sparkled as she touched the baby's cheek. "He's so soft, Mum," she spoke reverently. Elizabeth and George exchanged a parental glance of "this is a great moment."

Thomas skidded to an abrupt stop behind Desdemona. Rising on his tiptoes with arms spread wide, he avoided toppling over her.

"I wanna see. I wanna see!" He put his hands on her shoulders and shoved her aside.

"Thomas, you can't...!"

"It's fine, Father, I had my turn." Desdemona saved him.

"He looks like little Georgie, doesn't he, Mum? His hair sticks up a little in front just like mine. Do you suppose he will have freckles like me too? Can I hold him?"

Elizabeth placed the baby in his big brother's arms and cautioned, "careful, his head, you must support his head."

"I know, Mum." His grin was as wide as the London Bridge. "I'm your best brother you know." Thomas took a tiny hand in his and jiggled it as he chanted, "I'm your best brother. I'm your best brother."

Mary arrived, out of breath and out of patience. It seemed everyone on the deck wanted to talk about her mum and the new baby. "It's a boy and Mum is fine," she smiled at least a hundred times as she picked her way through the crowds and hurried down the stairs.

"You're his only brother," she teased, her blue-green eyes beaming. "Oh, Mum, he is so little. An angel of a boy!" She gave her mother a kiss on the forehead. "How are you feeling?"

"Fine dear. A bit tired, but fine."

"She'll be fine with some rest, I trust," George reassured his daughter. *What a beauty Mary Elizabeth is and she's only thirteen! She looks just like her mother and has the same kind disposition too.*

"I believe it's Mary's turn now." George carefully took the baby intending to pass him on, but intrigued by his delicate features and large blue eyes, held him for a long moment himself.

"Father, I thought it wa..."

"Oh, sorry Mary." He placed the baby in her arms and the children gathered in peering at his little face. They swayed back and forth to the rhythm that comes naturally when holding a new baby, occasionally faltering as the ship rolled in the high seas.

Chapter Two

The Blessing

Angel's Love Songs (3)

Their fourth night at sea had been a rough one with passengers made sick from the never ending rocking. It was Sunday and Elizabeth ailed as many others that night. George begged a bowl of broth from the ship's steward in the galley.

"Will you look at that, Betsy? It's the *S.S. Curling* etched right here on the bowl and the steward said we could keep it for baby Sanders, a birthday gift."[1] He tipped the bowl to her lips and she sipped gratefully, convinced that hot soup was all she needed to be well enough to attend her baby's blessing.

Putting all her weight on her arms, she lifted herself as she scooted off the bunk. Squatting down, she picked up her shoes, and set them on the bed. Cautiously she sat down and pulled them on. Her hair was up, the children were dressed, and the baby was tucked in the coverlet propped up on a pillow. His tiny face peeped out.

Mary picked him up and cradled him in her arms. "Ooh, baby Sanders. Aren't you a darling baby? Yes you are. Yes you are. Soooo Sweeeet."

Observing closely, Desdemona asked, "Why does Mary talk funny when she's holding baby Sanders?"

"I'm not sure," her mother answered, "but I think there's an unofficial language for talking to infants. It's how she says the words—almost like singing, that makes the difference. I've wondered if it might help babies learn to talk. I don't know, but it would sound odd to talk any other way to our wee ones." She gave Desdemona a quick hug. "Get your pinafore on now, dear, we must not be late!"

"George, can you get the new baby quilt out of the trunk for me?" Elizabeth asked, proud of her recent creation. She started it the day she felt the faint movement of new life inside her.

George hurried across the aisle and down three rows where their trunk was hidden under an enormous stack of belongings strapped to the walls. "Hmmmm. First the bundle," he muttered as he plopped the giant knapsack in the aisle. He shoved a wicker basket onto the adjacent stack. *Now get that case out of the way. Yes, there we go.* He set the old, brown leather case atop the wicker basket and opened his trunk. *Ah yes, there it is.* He rearranged the dishes and pots as he freed the quilt. "I've got it. Anything else you need?"

"No, just hurry. We mustn't be tardy." She steadied herself against the head post.

"Mary, bring me the babe, dear." Mary reluctantly gave the tiny child, warmly snuggled in her arms, to her mother who wrapped him in his Christening quilt.

It was a slow ascent for the Fox family with Elizabeth pausing every few stairs to catch her breath. She held her new baby tightly while George steadied her elbow as they climbed onto the deck.

"Hold on to her, George," Charlotte shouted as she hurried to meet them. "It's very slippery up here." They only saw her mouthed words above the roar. A wave crashed over the top of the bow and the ankle deep water rolled across the deck.

"Whoa, oh, oh, oh!" Sister Minor screamed as she slid by on her underskirts, feet up, arms flailing, eyes bulging. Brother Minor ran alongside trying to catch her.

Charlotte and George held on to Elizabeth, one on each side. Mary and Thomas held on to Desdemona who was laughing gleefully at the comedic scene.

The sisters' rounded knots of hair stayed in place, held fast by the holes in their elegant English bonnets, but the ornaments on their hats—feathers, pearls, ribbons and lace left long ago to ride the sea. Their dresses flapped about exposing their underskirts in a most shocking way. While busily holding down one side of their dresses, the wind would catch the other. Sister Tingey's bright pink dress flipped completely over her head exposing her broad backside. She was so distressed, her husband gave her smelling salts for she was sure she was going to faint. Desdemona put her hand over her mouth to cover her uncontrollable laughter. No one thought her rude because nothing could be heard above the whoosh and crash of the waves and the slapping of the sails against the masts. They pulled their woolen capes closed and gathered in clumps, the only protection from sudden gusts.

Thomas was glad he had two buttons left on his jacket. Some of the boy's jackets had no buttons so they had to choose whether to hold their hats over their ears or hold their jackets closed. Luckily they all had long sleeved shirts on and suspenders. At least they couldn't lose their pants, high water though they were.

The girls rolled the skirts of their pinafores up to their waists to make muffs for their cold hands and huddled together like new puppies. The deafening noise dared disruption by a human voice.

The meeting began with the prayer and hymn dissipating into the sea.

"We'll be blessing the new son of George and Elizabeth Fox this morning," Israel Barlow, former leader of the saints in Birmingham and Warwickshire, shouted above the roar. *(Angel's Love Songs–3)*

The saints gathered close creating an umbrella of protection from the blustering gale. George shielded the baby from the wind as he walked proudly to the front of the congregation. A few men joined him in a circle around the tiny newborn. Each placed his left hand upon the shoulder of the man next to him and extended his right arm to the middle of the circle forming a wheel. George's large hand held the baby in the middle. He began his humble address to God.

"Shorten the sail!" The abrupt order from Captain Curling passed through the first mate. "Shoooorten the saaaaail" echoed across the ship and the sailors began hauling down the out-rigged sails and adjusting the main topsail.

"Mr. Barlow." Heads turned to the direction of the demand. Israel Barlow raised his eyebrows, questioning. He thought he heard someone call his name.

"Mr. Barlow!" The captain was beside him now, still shouting. "The gale is increasing in strength; the waves will be crashing on the deck any moment. We are preparing for the worst. So, if you will take your people below we will batten down the hatches." Feet planted in a wide stance, his hands held behind him, he waited for nothing less than complete and immediate obedience.

Captain Curling had made many voyages across the expansive ocean without losing a single soul. A weather-beaten old tar, he knew well the fury of a raging storm and this one bore the earmarks of being the worst he had ever seen.

Israel Barlow looked past the saints that surrounded him. They too awaited a response. As he turned to meet the Captain's eyes a sense of calm was in his gaze. He respectfully, yet firmly stated, "The storm is nearly over, Captain, and it will not be increasing in violence. We will finish our meeting here." Their eyes fixed as each considered the other's position. Without further comment, Captain Curling wheeled abruptly and strode off.

The door to the Captain's cabin slammed open as the wind gave it an extra force yanking it from his heavy hand. He blustered and paced about his cabin. He studied his charts and analyzed his instruments. He tapped the eyeglass across his palm not sure of how to handle the situation. In all his years of sailing no one had ever dared challenge his orders and he was genuinely worried about his passengers' safety. Upon examination of his nautical instruments again, he noticed encouraging changes. He took the stairs two at a time, stood on the quarterdeck, and peered through his eyeglass.

"Well, I'll be a blue barnacle," he muttered. "It appears Mr. Barlow was right." The wind had subsided and the seas were calming.

He'd heard some seamen say they preferred having Mormons on board their vessels; they considered it a divine insurance of sorts. Before the Mormon migration began, from 1840 to 1851 there were 557 shipwrecks, mostly along the Atlantic coast, resulting in 655 deaths. While for the following thirty years only one ship wrecked with Mormons on it.[2] Captains and sailors attributed it to the common practice of the Mormons to dedicate the ship before sailing. Even though storms still raged, masts broke, and rigging fell, the vessels seemed to be granted the blessing of safe passage.

When the worship service closed with prayer, the seas were at peace. The gathering saints, who had moments before huddled for warmth and protection now strolled about the deck chatting in the afternoon sun.

"Thank you for a fine meeting, Elder Barlow. It was particularly important to my wife that our baby be blessed today." Elizabeth nodded in agreement.

"You are very welcome." Israel smiled broadly. Along with his unwavering faith and booming voice, his easy smile endeared him to his flock. He placed his hand on George's shoulder.

"We have had a witness here of the goodness of God." His voice was reverent, almost whispering, "for as I turned to the Captain's command, I saw scores of angels holding hands surrounding the ship."[3]

"Angels?" Elizabeth asked quietly.

"They were standing in the air completely surrounding us, holding hands. Their radiant whiteness is beyond description." He gazed past them, reliving the sacred experience. "I trust we shall make this voyage safely for the Lord is at the helm. He has protected us this day and will continue to do so."

His full gray beard lay upon his chest as he closed his eyes and bowed his head. The saints, within hearing, did likewise. Quietly they slipped away, hearts filled with thanksgiving.

Still weary from childbirth, Elizabeth leaned heavily on George as they descended the stairs one at a time.

"George," she spoke reverently, "We are blessed, you know. A new healthy babe and…" they stopped so she could catch her breath, "and, a miracle of angels at his blessing." She looked up at her husband and whispered, "I love you" and kissed his cheek.

Chapter Three

Land

Word traveled quickly of the sailor's call with its own distinct melody: "Land, ahoy!" The saints hugged the rail searching for a glimpse of shore. They had waited four weeks for the sight of land. Even though they valued the imensity of the sea, enjoyed the spouting whales, and reveled in the brilliant sunsets, their minds and hearts longed for earth and destination.

"Mum, there's land. I saw it." Thomas jumped on the bunk, landing on his knees at her feet. His mother looked up in amusement. "One of the sailors showed me. It's a thin gray line, and sometimes you can see it and sometimes you can't." Thomas glanced down at the floor with a contained grin. "Depends on how hard you squint and where you're looking from."

"Did he tell you when we'll dock? And," she paused, "I know that grin. *Where* were you looking from?"

"I climbed the rigging, half way up the main sail," he stammered, all but sure of her reaction.

Elizabeth sucked in her breath, ready to give her son a tongue-lashing. "What do you think you are doing climbing up…"

"I know, Mum, but it's safe enough, I promise, and I came directly to tell you, and everyone is up there watching."

His mother's eyebrows raised in disbelief.

"Oh, no, not on the rigging, Mum. Only a few of us got to do that! Just on the decks. Everyone's out on the decks."

Elizabeth had been dozing and not noticed that she and her baby were the only souls below deck. Even after four long weeks she still felt weak and her constant vigil was taking its toll.

"Come now Sanders, I'll carry you." He picked up the baby nestled in the blankets next to his mother. "Come little brother, we're going to see America!" Thomas held him on his shoulder with his hand cradling his head and sang cadences of "America, America," as they bounced together down the narrow aisles. Elizabeth tied the rose-colored hat ribbons under her chin as she followed with a quickened step to keep up with her sons.

"See that thin gray line over there?" George pointed out at sea.

"Where, Father? I just see water." Desdemona answered.

"Come up here." George patted his shoulder and hoisted her up. "Now can you see it?"

"Now I see even more water." She twisted so she could see all around her. "It's great up here, Father. There's a sea of colored hats. It's like a jiggley rainbow."

Two boys chased around George, grabbing his pant legs to steady themselves. "Hold on there lads!" He bent down and Desdemona slid safely onto the deck. The boys ran off and hid behind an enormous bright blue skirt. The woman, unaware of the safe haven she provided, chatted with her friend while energetically fanning herself.

"We're traveling by train first, I believe," she turned her head so her hat could provide much needed shade. "Then we're off to an outfitting town on the Missouri River. I can't remember which one. I think there are seventeen to choose from. I'll have to ask Elder Barlow, or," she thought for a moment, "I wonder if Charlotte Richards would know. After all, she's married to the man in charge of the whole emigration program in Great Britain. She ought to know." She scanned the deck. "Ah, there he is, talking to Sister Fox. Have you seen her new baby? Darling, absolutely darling." Her conversation mirrored others—travel plans, high hopes, new beginnings.

"It's good to see you, Sister Fox, Thomas," Elder Barlow greeted them and nodded as he tugged at his coat with both hands across his portly midsection.

The saints referred to each other with the terms "Brother" and "Sister" in reference to each person belonging to the Family of Man. Brother Israel Barlow, commissioned of Brigham Young to lead the saints on this voyage, was usually referred to as Elder Barlow, in reference to his official calling.

"Is it true? We shall be arriving soon?" asked Thomas.

"You'll be seeing the new emigration center before sundown, I'd say. Look for a round dome-shaped building on our port side as we enter the New York harbor. We'll dock at a pier near there. I always welcome the sight as a sign of new hopes and a new life."

"We shall welcome the sight, and certainly to set foot in America is most exciting!" Thomas nodded in agreement.

"Have you seen my dear husband?" She squinted, searching for his six-foot frame.

"Over there," Elder Barlow pointed starboard, "a bit past the main mast."

They found George with Mary leaning over the side as if getting a foot closer would make a difference in sighting the shoreline. Between them stood Desdemona stretched up on tiptoes with her chin resting on the rail and chattering like a magpie.

"I see it now, Father. See, Mum, that gray line is not just a line. It's America." She tugged on her mother's hand as a thousand questions ran through her mind and tumbled out of her mouth.

"Where will we sleep in America? How long will it take to get to the Great Salt Lake? Is it a real lake? Is it as big as the River Avon? Remember when we went there and had a picnic?"

"I do remember and I..." She tried to answer.

"How will our wagon carry all our things? How will we eat? Will there be Indians in New York? My friend Maude says she is afraid." Desdemona pointed to Maude who was across the deck swinging arms with her little sister.

"I'm not afraid." She paused, thought for a moment and admitted, "well, maybe a little bit afraid."

"Father, how will we carry all our bags?" She took a deep breath, "and those big trunks? Mum can't carry anything now, 'cept Baby Sanders." She looked up at her mother and smiled.

Elizabeth placed her hands on her daughter's shoulders and drew her close. Desdemona put her little finger near the baby's mouth to see if he would suck on it. She loved how his cute little bow-shaped mouth turned up in a sweet smile. "I could carry baby Sanders some of the way, couldn't I, Mum?"

"Of course, you can dear," Elizabeth answered kindly. "And, yes, the wagon will hold all of our things, at least, I think it will. You remember how big the wagon cover is? Your very own stitching on that canvas will help protect us." She paused, "but, most of all, dear, you must remember. We've come at the bidding of the Lord and we will be protected by His loving hands."

"And, we shall sleep on the ship for a night or two while the New York health inspectors give us an approval and the brethren can be notified of our arrival," George added.

"Will we meet the brethren then?" Elizabeth stated the question. "How long we have waited!"

"Some will be here. They've arranged for us to stay a few nights in Castle Gardens too, if needed, until we can make arrangements for our train passage to Pittsburgh."

"We're gonna see a castle, gonna see a castle, gonna..." Desdemona started singing.

"No, no, dear," her mother corrected. "It's not a castle; it's an old theater building that's been turned into an emigrant receiving station. The walls are covered with paintings." She continued, "so, it is kind of a garden, a garden of art."

"Oh, Father," Desdemona jumped up and down. "I will run off this ship with my fastest running feet and kiss the ground a hundred times, I will." She hugged her Father's legs.

Snickers and smiles surrounded the delightful child as she expressed the collective joy of the saints around her. All were anxious to get on to their Zion.

The gulls were flying low along the shore as the *S.S. Curling* slipped into New York Harbor at sunset on Tuesday, May 22, 1855.

Chapter Four

On to Kansas

The call of the gathering was urged in a letter issued from Brigham Young on December 23, 1847 requesting the Latter-day Saints to "bring utensils and machinery, and implements of any kind that would promote the comfort, health, happiness or prosperity of the people."

George packed his lamp-making tools along with one of his lamps. He wanted to bring his concertina, but sold it to increase their small savings for the long journey.

Elizabeth packed their belongings tenderly, giving thoughtful consideration to each item. She wrapped quilt squares around the dishes with blue Dutch windmills etched on them and placed them carefully in the wicker trunk. A wedding gift from her mother, the dishes were an heirloom from her grandmother Reid. All of the other items were of a more practical nature: pots, pans, clothing, a firearm, seeds, gardening tools, and buckets. Her hand-stitched quilts were layered among the belongings with the large family Bible wrapped in her favorite green quilt stitched with patterns of tulips.[4] Their precious Book of Mormon was on top for easy access. She even brought her small rocking chair that collapsed when a lever under the seat was pulled. Quite a clever contraption.

"Mum, when will we leave for Zion?" Mary anxiously twisted a strand of her hair around her finger, let it unwind, and twisted it again.

"I heard them say tomorrow." She whispered the answer, for her lips were close to the baby's ear as she hummed his favorite lullaby, "*A Mighty Fortress is Our God.*" Or, was it her favorite? *"O'er ills of life prevailing."* Whenever she was worried or uneasy she half sang, half hummed the words and melody slowly, over and over, revitalizing her faith and calming her fears.

They walked from the closest pier to Castle Gardens. Elizabeth rocked baby Sanders to sleep as she sat on one of the hard marble benches that circled the inside wall of the massive dome.

Beside her, Desdemona sat sprawled on the floor, legs spread wide with toes pointing up to the high ceiling. From above she looked like a generous serving of pie. She leaned forward with her elbows on the floor and her chin resting on her hands as she watched the steady flow of people. Her gaze followed a family of blue-eyed blondes until they vanished in the crowds. *Swedish, must be, with those embroidered aprons.* She wiggled her toes. *It's so noisy. I wonder if this is how the tower of Babel sounded?*

She sat up and stretched her arms over her head. *Look at all that plaid, must be a hundred Scots in that line. Mum loves plaid.*

"Ho there, Mum," Thomas yelled above the din.

It's Thomas! Desdemona sprang to her feet and promptly took her place on the bench with the other women of the family. Thomas often teased her about sitting like a boy. She smoothed her dress, straightened her back and sat regally with knees together and ankles crossed. Now she looked proper, well suited for a daughter of a fine Englishman.

"I'm ready to walk across those plains, just let me at 'em." Thomas hauled a satchel that was almost as big as he was. Trying to match his Father's footsteps, he would walk a few steps, and then would have to run to catch up. George resembled a traveling tinker with two trunks in each of his huge hands and a wicker basket balancing on his forearms.

"Whew, that was heavy and I'm starving." Thomas dropped his satchel near the pile of belongings that George had unloaded onto the bench. George dug deep in his pocket for a sea biscuit, found two, and gave one to Thomas.

"This will help." He seized the hard-crusted, saucer-shaped cracker and gnawed off a little piece, held it on his tongue to soften, then swallowed.

"We'll be leaving tomorrow, I expect." George said. He had attended the organizational meeting for the dispersal of the saints that morning. With soft eyes and a smile of admiration, she nodded as he explained, "we'll board the steamboat, 'Amboy' to Philadelphia, then we'll travel by rail to Pittsburgh."

"Father, Father, where will we sleep tonight?" Desdemona tugged hard at his elbow to get his full attention. Caught off balance as he bent down to slide the cumbersome basket onto the bench, she almost pulled him over.

"Watch yourself there, daughter. You'll sleep well on these benches. Mum's quilts will keep you just fine."

"Will you take me to see all the pictures, Father? Will you?" Desdemona, still attached to his arm, hopped up and down like a Mexican jumping bean. He placed his large hand over hers and looked thoughtfully at her freckled face.

"I will, dear," offered Elizabeth, knowing George had yet so much to do.

"And what about baby Sanders?" Desdemona asked. The baby cooed as if to say, "Yes, and what about me?" They all laughed and Elizabeth lifted Sanders above her head and gazed into his big blue eyes. The baby caught her nose and smiled. She turned her head playfully, allowing his hand to explore her face and sang, "We shall go a walking, a walking, a walking." She waltzed slowly around Desdemona. Mary joined them and held Sander's hand as she swayed to the self-made music. Desdemona caught hold of the baby's foot and giggled. Her laughter was contagious.

How beautiful they are! And, what a blessed man I am! Amused and disarmed by his lovely wife and daughters, George smiled with satisfaction.

"I'll take care of the baby." Mary held her arms out and the baby smiled. "Go on Mum, have a wonderful time."

Elizabeth held Desdemona's hand and they strolled through Castle Gardens swinging their arms and laughing like school children as they admired the bright palette of paintings and people around them.

Mary, the practical caretaker, questioned her Father as she laid Sanders across her knees and patted his back, "and from Pittsburgh, Father? Where do we go from Pittsburgh?"

"We board the steamship, *Amazon* and go on to St. Louis, if all goes as planned." George's eyes twinkled as he tousled her hair and grabbed Thomas' half-eaten sea biscuit.

"That's if we don't starve to death first." He laughed as he put his arms around their shoulders and hugged them to him.

Chapter Five

The Departure

Children of Light (4)

Elizabeth shaded the baby's eyes as she stooped to lay him in the hand-carved cradle that George had given her. They were camped about five miles west of Atchison, Kansas, on the banks of the Missouri River. She looked across the sea of grass dotted with bustling people, open mouthed wagons, and lazy animals as she rocked the cradle gently with her foot hoping the movement would lull her son to sleep. *(Children of Light–4)*

"Mama, he's so beautiful," Mary said, as she bent over the cradle. "He must be so exhausted in this heat." She touched his cheek and tried to elicit his familiar and most adorable smile. "Poor little fellow. I hope those pesky mosquitoes don't get you, baby. I'll keep them away…yes, I will…I'll take care of you." She talked softly but he didn't respond. "Is something wrong with Sanders, Mum?" She held her hand against his cheek. "He always smiles when I talk to him."

"He's not been nursing well and I am worried. Does he feel warm to you? Of course, it's so warm today it feels like everyone has a fever."

George surveyed their stacks of misshapen belongings with a critical eye and a wrinkled brow. "What to put in first?" George asked himself as he stroked his beard.

"Betsy, what d' you think of our new prairie schooner?"

"Hmmmm." was the only answer he received. Lately, Elizabeth's focus on her newborn had reduced her responses to this brief acknowledgement.

"Mary, help me with the cover, will you?" Thomas called. "It takes two people to cover a wagon." She ran to the wagon and caught the cascading blanket of canvas. "Pull it tight and lash it down." Thomas instructed her from the other side of the wagon. Because of his keen interest, he had learned quickly as he watched other families prepare for the trek.

"I can't see where to hook it," she muttered, concentrating on pulling and searching at the same time. Here it is!" Her mother hurried over, pulled the canvas taut and helped Mary lash it to the wagon side.

"That's the last one." Thomas sauntered around the wagon, looking over his achievement. "Now, we'll, just thread the rope through the casing in the back and we've got a real, covered wagon." He laughed as he dusted his hands off just like his Father, a signal of work well done.

"Oh, wait!" Elizabeth turned to Thomas. "Before you pull the back closed, will you help your Father with the loading?"

She was proud of her children. Tom's independent and adventurous nature fit the demands of this rugged country and Mary was like having a second pair of hands. If it wasn't for Mary...well, she didn't know what she would do. Desdemona relished every discovery, from the colorful wild flowers to the multi-legged bugs crawling on the prairies. She was delightful, chattering and singing most of the day. Like a bright sunflower swaying in a gentle breeze, she lifted the spirits of all around her. It was her gift.

Elizabeth walked between the stacks with her hands on her hips as she surveyed the heaps. "Hmmmmm." She stopped by a chimneystack of boxes. "Charlotte told me yesterday the best way to start loading is to divide everything into three piles. Memorabilia—most of ours is in the wicker trunk—things we'll need when we get there, like your tools and my quilting frames," she paused for breath, which she was often short of these days, "then all of the food and clothing we'll need along the way, and of course our bedding on top."

Stooping down to pick up a bag of oatmeal, Elizabeth thought better of it and smiled as she sauntered over to her handsome husband, put her arms around his waist and buried her head in his chest. Her squeeze sent a silent message.

"Ah, Betsy," he held her close and spoke into her hair. "I love you, too, I do."

A faint cry escaped the cradle, which soon would be a full-blown bawl if she didn't hurry. She didn't want him to waste his energy on crying, for he had little to spare. She picked him up as Captain Milo Andrus called to her husband.

"How're you doing there, Brother Fox?" hailed the Church appointed wagon master. He rode the only horse on the wagon train, a chestnut colored roan of magnificent proportions.

George and Thomas had just lowered one of the fifty pound barrels of flour onto the wagon floor as Captain Andrus approached.

"How was your training this morning?" he asked with a wry smile. He had watched the teamsters test their newly learned techniques of driving a team. It was quite a sight, with all the "greenhorns" trying to catch and yoke their oxen. The air was filled with the sounds of cracking whips and loud shouts of "Gee" to get the beasts to go from them and "Haw" to come towards them.[5]

"I s'pose I'll get it soon enough."

"We'll be meetin' at eight in the morning for prayer before headin' out." He tugged on the reigns, spurred the horse with his heels, and galloped to the next wagon.

They packed tirelessly. With three hundred pounds of breadstuffs per person, plus all of their belongings, their wagon was bulging by dusk. They would have to get up at sunrise to harness the oxen. Even though they practiced, they could count on an extra measure of frustration as the huge creatures were not known to be overly cooperative.

Elizabeth slept little as she tried to nurse her baby throughout the night. She applied the cool compresses that Charlotte gave her, but the symptoms of milk fever didn't subside.

At dawn she looked with weary eyes at her tiny baby turning and twisting at her breast seeking nourishment. His frustrated cries were barely audible, a quiet whimpering.

Please, help him to nurse, she prayed silently. *Please, please help me.*

"There, there," she whispered as she cradled his head in her hands and bounced him gently. "Don't cry." She cuddled him close and tried nursing again.

"It will be all right. I promise. Don't cry, my little one, don't cry," she pleaded as tears ran down her cheeks.

When the baby finally suckled, pain stabbed through to her spine. Even so, she was relieved because he was warm and he was feeding. She rocked and listened as the camp began to stir.

"How's the babe today, Betsy? Did you get any sleep?" George kissed her on the cheek and tenderly stroked the baby's head.

"The baby nursed and that's good and, no, I didn't get much sleep but enough to last me I think." She smiled. "Go on, dear. Don't worry about me. I'll have some biscuits ready shortly." He raised his eyebrows. "Mary will help me, I'll be fine."

George strode around the wagon rousing the children. "Thomas, get hold of that barrel and we'll strap it on." They worked together, fine-tuned to each other's movements. "That's the end of it." George muttered under his breath and brushed his hands together in a gesture of finality.

Thomas, normally not all that demonstrative, threw his hat high in the air with a "Yippee!" The whole family stared in disbelief. He grinned. "It means best and wonderful mixed together. And that's how I feel because I'm going to walk to Zion. Why, I might even run!" Since leaving England, freckles had popped out on his tanned face and his already high-water trousers were now even shorter. His floppy hat, purchased in St. Louis, and red plaid shirt made him the perfect American pioneer.

"What a funny word, Yippee," declared Mary, always a bit more serious than her siblings. "Feels funny when you say it. Don't you think it's a funny…" She stopped in mid-sentence as she glanced at her mother. Elizabeth's head drooped and the baby was sound asleep lying across her knees.

"Oh, Mum." Quietly Mary lifted baby Sanders from her lap. Elizabeth looked up.

She shrugged her shoulders, peeled herself from the rocking chair and answered the inquisitive looks. "I'm fine, just a bit tired." She yawned. "Best get our little Sanders into his cradle, and I surely want this chair to be atop that load." She stood straight, chin held high, defiantly dispelling any sign of fatigue. "We'll need it in Zion."

George wedged the heirloom rocker in a crevice that would hold it straight while they traveled. "There you go, Betsy, all set. And, I can easily remove it in the evenings so you can rock by the campfire."

Elizabeth smiled. "Thank you dear." She climbed up and settled herself into the rocker. Mary put baby Sanders, still sleeping inside the cradle, into the wagon and joined her mother on the perch. Desdemona skipped alongside her father and brother as they managed the oxen.

On that hot August morning the Milo Andrus Company of 456 souls, 48 wagons, 262 oxen, 60 cows, one horse, one mule and one piano set out as one of the last wagon trains heading west in 1855.[6] Children ran beside the wagons, playing games of tag and foot race. The young men lengthened their strides to keep up with the oxen and the calls of "haw" and "gee" resounded along the trail. Excitement and billows of dust filled the air.

Chapter Six

The Trek

Square Dance (5) followed by *Quilters (6)*

"My feet hurt, Mum," moaned Desdemona. She spent her days picking wild flowers and wading through the tall grasses of the Nebraska plains. Even though it was fun to romp alongside the wagon, her feet knew when they had walked their daily quota of fifteen miles.

"Come up here and ride with me." Her mother patted the wooden plank next to her.

"No, the bumps are too hard." She shook her head and instinctively rubbed her hip, remembering the ride on the perch a couple of days before. No, it didn't take much thought to decide that it was more comfortable to walk.

So far their travels had been without incident. The tracks were wide and deep as the trail led northwest to hook up with the Mormon Trail near the North Platte River. At last night's camp Captain Andrus met with the 'Captains of Ten' and gave each a copy of "The Latter-day Saints Emigrants Guide: being a Table of Distances from Council Bluffs to the Valley of the Great Salt Lake" by William Clayton. His careful measuring with his "mile machine" marked by the rotations of a wagon wheel helped the wagon trains find the next water source. The book's clear and detailed descriptions of landmarks and detailed topography proved to be an invaluable asset.[7]

George read his copy with great interest. As a 'Captain of Ten,' it was his responsibility to keep his assigned ten wagons together. If one of them had trouble, all ten stayed with that wagon until they could go on as a group and catch up to the main body of the wagon train.

Brother Andrus waved his hat as he rode by, the signal that they would be circling up in the next clearing. Their wagons slowed and the process of settling in for the night began.

"When's supper? I'm so hungry I could eat a buffalo tongue smothered in grasshopper juice." He watched his mother wince. Thomas was always hungry. Elizabeth heard somewhere that there was a primeval curse of eternal hunger that affects all boys at the age of ten and lasts until they are sixty. She believed it!

"Soon, I expect." Elizabeth was going to fix a stew with beans and a bit of the antelope meat left from yesterday. She missed the potatoes and leeks of England although, she was adjusting to the rigors of camp cooking and, according to George, she did make a tasty antelope stew.

"I'm starvin'." The physical labor and fresh air of the plains agreed with Thomas. He'd grown taller and filled out, but his boyish grin…it stayed the same, as wide as ever.

"Please get the rocking chair down for me before you and Father take the oxen to pasture, will you Thomas?" Elizabeth thought in multiples, not only what she needed to do, but also what tasks each child needed to do to settle in for the night. Setting up camp was a family affair.

"Mary, hold the babe until I can get supper on." While giving directions, she reached in the wagon box for the large iron kettle, dug through a bag for potatoes and tore off a piece of the dried antelope meat.

"Desdemona, pull out the quilts and please don't drag them across the ground. Give them a good shaking then fold them up and stack them in the back of the wagon."

She smiled as she watched her children perform their duties. They didn't need her coaching, but it felt good to Elizabeth to be in control. Other than her difficulty in nursing and feeling a bit dizzy now and then, she was satisfied with their travels thus far. She did worry about the baby though. He slept long hours at a time and seemed listless. She could coax a smile once in a great while, but the spontaneous smile that used to make the family laugh was gone. And, he felt warm, always warm.

"Well, Betsy!" George was sitting on the wagon tongue with his empty cup in his hands. "That was a mighty fine stew." He hesitated, turned his head where he thought she wasn't looking and spat on the ground. *(Square Dance–5)*

Elizabeth frowned. "George!" She hated the new habit he'd acquired on the frontier. He shrugged his shoulders and grinned.

"I think we'll all have to do some high steppin' tonight." He winked at his wife, sauntered over, and scooped her up in his arms holding her like a baby as he turned round and round.

"Trying to live up to your reputation as the best step dancer from Birmingham, my husband?" Elizabeth teased as she kissed his cheek and slid to the ground.

"No, no." George shook his head with a twinkle in his eye, "certainly not. Would I do such a thing? Seriously, I think it's time for our tall Thomas to put his young legs to a few steps."

"Aw, Father, it looks too hard," Thomas mumbled as he kicked a small rock rolling in the dirt. "I don't know how t'dance."

"I'll teach you and your Father can teach Mary," Elizabeth directed.

"And who will watch the baby?" Mary looked up from the baby, her fingers still held in his small fist.

"I will, I will. I can take the cradle and sit on the sides. Please, Mum?" Desdemona ran over to Mary and sat down by the cradle. "I can watch him, huh, Mary?" She needed her sister's allegiance.

"What do you think, Father?"

Elizabeth was hesitant. *Sanders hasn't nursed well for several days and looks a bit pale. He did smile this afternoon though.* She wondered.

"Can't be any harm in trying." George handed Desdemona a small plaid blanket. "Wave this if you need us. I'll help you carry the cradle over and get you situated."

"If he gets fussy, dear, wave the blanket, and I'll come straight away," her mother added.

"So, ready yourselves for the dance." George turned to his son. "Thomas, you too!"

The fiddlers played for a couple of hours. The women's dresses swished and the men's heels beat intricate patterns into the dusty ground. They were happy to follow the advice of Brigham Young who, on his trek west, said, "There is no harm in dancing. The Lord said to praise Him in all things. Thank the Lord in prayer afterwards for the privilege of dancing and ask for his blessings on the camp."

The Fox family danced and laughed as they traded partners regularly. The rigors of the day were forgotten as they enjoyed the strains of the violin and mouth harp. The wagons that had been stuck up to their hubs in mud had been recovered and the herds of oxen, cattle, and sheep grazed on the high Nebraska grass. The hot August day cooled and all found refreshment in the dance. Enthusiastic onlookers clapped and stomped to the lively tunes.

Elizabeth looked over at Desdemona sitting by the cradle rocking it to the rhythm of the music. She knew Desdemona would be attentive, but a gnawing concern persisted. *Is Sanders really all right?* Desdemona caught her glance, grinned and waved.

Thomas guided his mother into the throng of dancers. He was learning quickly to take the lead. She faltered, and they both nearly fell into Brother and Sister Roylance.

"You all right, Mum? I'm sorry. Are you all right?" Thomas asked his mother.

"Fine, I'm fine. I must have got off a bit," she reassured him although she wasn't so sure herself. She felt light headed.

"I think I'll sit out the next one, son." She leaned heavily on his arm as he guided her through the crowd.

"Desdemona," he called to her as they approached. "Meet us at the wagon!"

"But, Thomas, I..." Startled, she looked up, but couldn't see him anywhere. She raised the corner of the quilt to check on the sleeping baby then carefully lifted the cradle, keeping it level so he wouldn't wake up. She hastened past the onlookers and around the wagons.

Thomas helped his mother into the rocker, laid a quilt across her lap and waited, pacing to the end of the wagon, then to his mother, back and forth. *Hurry Desdemona, hurry. I can't leave Mum alone.* He paced faster trying to calm his nerves.

Finally his sister emerged from the wagon silhouettes. Patting his mother's hand, he kissed her forehead as a hasty goodbye. She smiled and nodded.

"I'm going to find Father," Thomas yelled over his shoulder, "take care of Mum!"

Desdemona let out a deep sigh as she placed the cradle by her mother's chair. Her arms ached and she was out of breath.

"What happened? You all right, Mum?"

"Of course dear, I just got a bit unsettled. That's all. I'm quite all right. And, how is our baby Sanders?" *(Quilters–6)*

"Still sleeping. I don't know how he sleeps through all that noise. It is so exciting. I love the clapping and the stomping and the swishing dresses. I put a quilt over the cradle so the mosquitoes couldn't get him and he fell asleep. Fell asleep! Just like that!" She snapped her fingers and smiled at herself. She'd been practicing since the day they left the flatboat.

Elizabeth, too tired to respond, closed her eyes and breathed out a, "Hmmmmm."

I'll rest a little. This will pass. All things pass. I am a little weak, but enduring, that's the key. Rest and endure. She leaned back in her rocking chair.

Desdemona worried, unaware that she was rocking the cradle to the rhythm of the music. *Mum is so tired. I wish Thomas would hurry.*

Heart pounding and stomach knotted, Thomas hunted for his Father's familiar plaid shirt. His mother had made him one out of the same fabric so it was easy to remember. He spotted Mary and his Father visiting with a couple of brethren.

"I can help you with that, Brother LeRandall. Bring your son in a few…"

"Father," Thomas was out of breath. "Mum's sick."

"Where is she?"

"At the wagon, with Desdemona."

George rushed past Thomas and pushed through the crowds with an occasional, "Pardon me." Elizabeth's health had concerned the family from the day they rolled out of Kansas. She insisted the dizzy spells had subsided.

They found her slowly rocking with her head leaned back and her eyes closed. Father and son lifted her into the wagon and placed baby Sanders beside her. They prayed together and continued with silent prayers long after she slept.

Days passed and Elizabeth's body demanded rest even though her heart and mind were full of faith. She recalled the words from last night's prayer meeting. Captain Andrus held his Book of Mormon high in the air and admonished the saints to keep in their minds and hearts the reason for their journey. They needed to remember their Savior and his great sacrifice. They could rely on Him in faith to bless them.

Morning brought renewed commitments from the saints, lighter burdens. Brighter countenances—as they remembered.

Elizabeth lay in the wagon with her baby. Amidst the dust and noise her thoughts remained focused on the tiny fellow at her bosom. He didn't search for her as before. He had no appetite.

"Wake up, little fellow," she shook him gently. "Come my little one, you need to eat."

Weak with exhaustion and feeling unusually warm, Elizabeth rode on trying to find comfort in the rhythmic jostling of the wagon. She clutched her baby tightly to console him, and herself, as she hummed the hymn that so often brought her solace.

She fought off the waves of doubt that plagued her. *Is it my imagination or is Sanders lighter now than when we docked in New York?* She unwrapped the blankets to look at him. *He's so small, but his belly is large. Those tiny legs, they're so thin. I better have Charlotte look at him. She'll know what to do. She always knows.* He slept on as she wrapped him again and held him close. The bellowing of the oxen and the jostling of the wagon kept her from feeling his warm breath on her cheek.

"Betsy," Charlotte, walking alongside the wagon, interrupted her thoughts. "Do you have a pinch of salt I could borrow? Well, no, I mean could you give me a pinch for, you know, I can't return it 'til we get to Salt Lake." They slowed to a stop for the noon hour meal.

"Oh, Charlotte, I'm so glad to see you." She struggled to support herself on her elbow to see her sister-in-law and dearest friend. "I'm worried about baby Sanders. Will you have a look?"

"Ah, such a wee one, Betsy." Charlotte stood by the wagon. Elizabeth felt fortunate that Charlotte was the caretaker of the wagon train. Though not officially trained in the art of medicine, her knowledge of herbs and liniments surpassed most.

She summoned all her energy to climb down from the wagon so Charlotte could get a closer look. She bent over the babe and put her cheek to his face. The air was still. She looked into Elizabeth's eyes and they both knew.

Elizabeth caught her breath. "Noooooooooo..." The protest poured from her soul. "Not again. Please not again." She picked up the baby, held him on her shoulder and patted his back like she had a hundred times before.

"Betsy!" George ran to her. "Betsy."

She sobbed. "He's gone!" George wrapped his arms around her as she held the baby's face close to hers.

"There's...no...breath." She held the baby out for George but as he reached for the small bundle, she jerked away, clutching her Sanders tighter. She fiercely rocked from side to side as if the movement would give her baby life.

"It's all right Sanders. You'll be all right." Elizabeth spoke softly. "Wake up my little one. Wake up now, my son. You're going to be fine, just fine."

Mary and Thomas ran to their Father. They felt his tears wet their hair as they clung together. Charlotte found Desdemona a few wagons away and held her close as she told her that her baby brother had gone to live with Jesus.

Elizabeth fell to her knees in the tall grass and rocked her baby Sanders with her whole body. Then, bending to the earth she carefully rewrapped the lifeless child, caressing his face with her fingers, and softly expressing her love. For a long time, she cradled him in her arms, kissing his nose and his cheeks, again and again.

She was calm when she held him in front of her to look once more at his sweet face, and then, slowly, with both hands, with resolve to accept this trial, she lifted him high in the air. The blanket fell open and her gaze remained fixed on the heavens as tears streamed their familiar paths down her cheeks and on to the prairie.[8]

Chapter Seven

Elizabeth

Dance with Your Treasures (7) followed by *Mourning (8)*

It was twilight when they buried the tiny babe under a small grove of trees. His body was wrapped in the quilt made by his mother barely a year ago. The service was short and poignant.

"We are all saddened by little Sander's passing but his very innocence will bring him eternal joy." Brother Andrus spoke to the parents and friends who had gathered by the gravesite.

"He now abides in the loving arms of the Savior." A few saints bobbed their heads in silent agreement. "Celestial glory is his everlasting blessing. Yet, we mourn. And, the scriptures tell us to mourn with those that mourn and bear one another's burdens that they may be light. May we be at peace as the Comforter attends us and we attend each other." They returned to their wagons with renewed resolve to love, to care, to comfort.

Night brought wandering thoughts and fitful sleep for the Fox family, especially Elizabeth. She fought the covers, thrashing and turning, denying her deepest knowledge. Her hair lay in wet ringlets on her forehead. The infection that had prevented her from nourishing her baby now ravaged her body. She felt the full effects of milk fever — loss of appetite, bouts of spiked fever, delirium, and overwhelming fatigue.

Mary took over the cooking with help from Charlotte. On the difficult days, the children took turns caring for their ailing mother. Desdemona gathered the buffalo chips for the fire then sat holding her mother's hand while dispensing unceasing chatter of the day's events. Thomas kept the oxen in line and loaded and unloaded the necessities for daily camp. For the most part, their mother was content to sit in her wedged rocking chair and watch the dusty plains along the North Platte River slowly go by.

At night, George would lie with his arms around her until she fell asleep. It was in the depths of sleep that she called out to her baby and George would soothe her with loving words of comfort.

Some days Elizabeth functioned well, giving hope to her family that the illness was past. She laughed as Desdemona sang "Pop goes the Weasel" when they passed through a prairie dog town where hundreds of brown furry creatures stood like sentinels by their holes. The children tried to catch them but the little barking dogs would quickly dive into their burrows, only to pop up again somewhere else.

She gave thanks with the rest of the camp at the sight of buffalo for she knew that meant meat for their pots. Her awareness was keener as Chimney Rock appeared on the horizon. The halfway mark to the Great Salt Lake, the unique rock formation resembled the factory smokestacks of Liverpool and could be seen from a distance of forty-two miles through a glass. When they camped across from Scott's Bluffs, she rocked and stared at the wind carved rocks shaped like the spires and arches on the castles in England.

Days later, she hiked, albeit slowly, to Independence Rock, a rounded mass of granite over one hundred feet high and covering about three acres. She and the girls swatted mosquitoes as they sat on the rocks below while George and Tom scratched *Fox–1855* into an open space between *Pratt–1848* and *Simpson–1852.*[9] The descent from the continental divide in Wyoming was a harrowing one, but, at last they arrived in the Green River Valley. The thick cottonwood trees along the Green River were a welcome change from the dry, barren plains. *(Dance with Your Treasures–7)*

"Go get the baby, dear." Elizabeth smiled and stirred the supper stew.

"Yes, Mum." Mary walked to the other side of the wagon as she had every day for almost nine weeks now. Elizabeth smiled, pleased that her daughter was so helpful.

"That stew sure smells great, Ma." Thomas had long since changed "Mum" for "Ma." His mother hadn't noticed.

"It will be just fine," was her quiet response. She methodically went about her duties of setting for supper. They ate, they talked, they cleaned up.

"How is my brother's family this fine evening?" Charlotte was given a warm reception as she dished out hugs like her famous apple cobbler, sweet and satisfying.

"Just fine." George was happy to see her. As a captain, he often had meetings after supper, so he missed her daily visit. He relied heavily on her to watch over Elizabeth.

"Aunt Charlotte, I need to fix this tear in my apron but I can't find our sewing box." Mary stuck her finger through the hole as she talked.

"I'll bring mine right over. I'm sure I have some green thread in there somewhere." She draped her arm on Mary's shoulder and discretely guided her away from the wagon as they talked. "So, how is your Mum doing today?"

"The same. Your plan still works. I pretend to get the baby and when I come back she thinks everything is fine."

"Good," she nodded. "Good."

"Will she ever stop looking for him?" Mary's wrinkled brow showed her concern.

"Not until her heart has healed and her fever is completely gone and presently, she's still warm to my touch."

"Is there anything else we can do?" George joined them. "You know, I found her yesterday by the Adams' wagon looking for the baby again. She mourns terribly." George shook his head and let out a deep, ragged breath. "She mourns hard, Charlotte. I just don't know how to help her."

Charlotte put her hand on his arm. "I've given her every herb tea I know of. The compresses seem to be helping, but that's all I know to do. Just humor her so she'll stay calm. You must be patient."

"Oh, I know you are." She admired George and didn't want him to think otherwise. "Time is her friend. She will heal."

"We surely thank you, Charlotte. Don't know what we would..." George's words wouldn't come. He hugged her. No words were needed.

"Father, I hear the violin. Can we go now?" Desdemona said sweetly, tugging on his arm. She looked up, her soft green eyes pleading. Her Father could not resist. Besides, he thought the event might be good for all of them. "Go get your mother."

George glanced at the campfire. "Comin' Charlotte?" The day's journey seemed lighter as they expended every last drop of energy clapping and dancing. Even Elizabeth enjoyed the fun. For a brief moment her grief was forgotten. *(Mourning–8)*

That night the saints slept soundly. They didn't hear the winds whistling through their camp. The winds always blow in Wyoming. They didn't hear the gurgling of the swift current that had filled their water barrels that day. And, they didn't hear a baby's haunting cries or the fleeing footsteps through their camp.

Is that you Sanders? Don't cry. She carefully moved George's hand from her waist and sat up. *I'll bring your blanket to you.* Clutching the small plaid blanket to her chest, she froze. Listening. Her heart pounded. *Sanders, don't cry my baby, I'm coming.* Mary turned over and coughed. Elizabeth waited. No one moved as she crawled to the back of the wagon and climbed down. Even her low moan as she fell to the ground wasn't heard.

"My sweet baby, where are you?" she whispered. She looked under their wagon, then scurried to the next. A horse whinnied. Startled, she dropped to her hands and knees and crawled across the cold, parched ground, over the prickly sagebrush and dried grass, away from the camp. She stopped and sat by a large boulder near the trail. She spread her baby's blanket on the ground.

"I'm ready for you," she pleaded. She crept around the rock groping for her baby. "I have your blanket." She whispered as she folded it carefully and rocked it in her arms. "Where are you little one? Are you hungry?" She stood up. The blanket fell from her arms and she caught it in her fist. Her shoulders drooped. Her head was cocked to one side. Her hair hung limp across her eyes and the blanket hung at her side.

His crying beckoned her. Her mind screamed. *I'm coming, my baby, I'm coming!*

Her hair flew as she ran across the prairie. The black sky with millions of pinpricks aided her hazed vision.

Frantically, she plunged through a patch of wild berry bushes ignoring the thorns that pierced her flesh and ripped her dress. She pushed the branches aside with bleeding hands as she smiled and half whispered loving messages in the dark.

Her smile brightened. *I'll find you. Please don't cry. You're probably over in those shadows. Yes, that's where you are! You're under the trees. I'm coming.* She darted down the slope to the riverbank where a grove of cottonwood trees created webs of leaves above her. She searched, oblivious to the sharp cuts and scratches inflicted by the unforgiving underbrush.

"I hear you my little one. I'm here for you." Her voice was thin and high, her feverish eyes were glazed over, and her face was wet with sweat. Delirium gave way to exhaustion.

Humming her favorite lullaby, she meandered into the thick mass of organ pipe-like reeds that swallowed her as they easily gave way to her slender body. Like a tall cornfield maze, she became invisible under the cover of leaves. "I'm here, dear one, I'm here for…" She stumbled on a jagged rock, her knees buckled, and she crumbled to the ground. She lay there. Still. Clutching the plaid blanket to her bosom.

Her body found peace in the depths of sleep but her mind still searched, for she could see him, in his cradle, his eyes closed, sucking on his tiny hands. She heard his soft whimpers with each short intake of breath as she knelt beside him and reached down to take him in her arms. Almost…, she almost touched him.

Chapter Eight

George

As if in a fog, they walked together, arm in arm down the wide city streets. The mercantile displayed its wares: fancy dresses, velvet hats, leather vests. "Which one would you like, my dear, the purple or the emerald green that matches your eyes?" Her face was radiant as she stood before him in the green brocade dress. The ecru lace gathered down the front made a slender V accenting her tiny waist. They embraced and he tenderly kissed her on the lips. "Let me look at you." He held her hand in his as she stepped back and curtsied. "Ah, you look so beautiful, Betsy." She looked into his eyes.

"So beautiful, Betsy." George mumbled in his sleep. He reached for her. His open hand pressed flat against the quilt. It took several moments for his fingers to detect her absence. "Betsy?" Startled, he sat up.

"Betsy!" He shouted as he pulled on his boots and grabbed his jacket.

"Mary, Thomas, get up."

"Wha…" Thomas was a slow riser. "It's not time to…"

"Your mother's gone!" He was already walking to the next wagon. "I'm going to check with your Aunt Charlotte. I've got to see if your Mum's there. Mary, get Desdemona ready and bring her over."

He walked in long hurried strides, his eyes combing the landscape for any sign of Betsy. His mind raced. *Where would she go? We've always found her before. She can't be far.*

"Charlotte!" he started calling long before he arrived. "Charlotte?"

She poked her head out the back of her wagon. "George, is that you…?"

"She's gone. Betsy's gone!" His face was ashen and his hands trembled.

"I'll be right out." Charlotte wrapped a blanket about her and climbed down. "How long? Are you sure she isn't about the camp somewhere?"

"I've been calling her." He surveyed the area as he answered. The camp was just beginning to stir: men laying the fires, yawning and stretching before a hard day's work, women shaking out the blankets and giving orders, children chattering. His eyes scrutinized each family, hoping to see his wife among them.

"Mary's bringing Desdemona over. I knew this would happen. I usually stay awake until she's fallen asleep and I thought I did last night." He shook his head in disbelief. "I don't know, I just don't know."

"Don't you worry now, George. We'll find her. Get yourself going that way." She pointed to the Hanks' wagon west of them. "And I'll go over to the Adams' and the Walkers'. We've found her before, it'll be all right." Her voice trailed as George headed off.

"Where's Father going?" Mary held Desdemona's hand. "Is my Mum here?"

They read the answer on her face. Her arms opened wide and they ran to her. Desdemona clung to her skirt. "We'll find her, girls. We'll find her. Your Father's gone to get Captain Andrus. We'll find her."

Thomas nervously poked around their camp looking everywhere he could think of. His Father had told him to stay there, so he did, sort of. He went to the Stevenson's wagon and roused them out of their sleep asking if they'd seen his mum.

He kept thinking of the night before, how they had danced and then, after family prayer, she had looked him in the eye and said, "Son, I'm so proud of you. You're a fine young man of Zion, you are." Then she added, poking her finger at his chest, "not a great dancer yet, mind you, but it will come. Now go say your prayers and get some sleep." They laughed.

"Any sign of her, Thomas?" George, astride the large roan, pulled up short. Thomas shook his head. He looked scared. The spirited horse pranced about as his Father continued, "Captain Andrus is organizing a search. We're meeting in the clearing." He pointed to the open space on the rise about a hundred feet from them. "Grab some biscuits and meet me over there."

After a quick prayer, Captain Andrus divided the search parties putting the Captains of Ten in charge.

"Brother Matthews, you go downriver. Hopefully you can make it to the bend and back before supper."

"Brother Dean, take your men upriver to the cliff point, 'bout three miles north."

"Brother John, you're the best tracker here, so you start at the Fox's wagon and fan out in a circle heading southeast so as not to miss any sign." John Duncan nodded his head in agreement. His expertise in tracking gave George hope.

"If you find her, fire off a shot as a signal."

"Come on brethren, let me show ya how to look for sign." The men pressed in as John knelt on one knee and showed them the finer points of tracking.

"I'll need your men," Milo faced Brother Scott, "to follow the river bank. Wade out where you can. Look for any sign of Indians."

"Jeremiah, did you see anything unusual last night?" Milo questioned. "Weren't you and William on watch?"

"Yes Sir. But it was all quiet, far as I could tell." He continued, "like I told you this mornin', Captain, the cattle were spooked and I thought I saw something move, but when I went over there to look, there wasn't anybody there."

"I know, I looked it over and couldn't see anyone either," William Todd spoke up. "Nothin' happened on my watch, Sir." William, a thin, willowy lad was particularly concerned. He had come over on the *S. S. Curling* and Thomas was his best friend.

"So be it." Milo, puzzled, pushed his hat back and scratched his balding head. "Cut down the brush if you have to. It's so thick a grasshopper couldn't hop through it."

"George." He laid his hand on George's shoulder. "We'll find her. The only direction we haven't covered is northeast. I'm thinking she might have gone back on the trail we came in on. Here, take my glass." He handed the valuable tube to George.

George stuck it in his belt and started walking. "Let's fan out past those oxen." He pointed to the open field where the herds were grazing.

The men lumbered off in their appointed directions. The sounds of scythes meeting reeds, the tinkling of cowbells and echoes of "Elizabeth" bounced off the high cliffs across the river.

The search continued through the noonday meal and on past supper. Hungry and tired, each search party returned to camp thinking the other had probably found her. Hopes dwindled but resolve remained. They would look again tomorrow. The October night seemed colder as thoughts and prayers were offered. All the ages ached together for the lost Elizabeth, for the children, and for George.

"They will find her tomorrow."

"Your Mum will be fine."

"She can't have gone far."

"Here's my best marble. I'm sorry 'bout your ma."

And, so it went. Surely another day of searching and praying would result in a happy reunion. But, the next day brought no Elizabeth, although Brother Matthews found several small footprints near the river about a mile downstream where it extended across eighty feet. George went to see for himself.

George slept little that night. His mind went over and over the possibilities. *I think those are her footprints. She's afraid of the water. It's cold tonight. It's going to get colder. She can't swim. We're low on supplies. I've held them up two days already. I can't risk their lives.* His skin crawled with gooseflesh. *She's got to be alive. She's asleep. She was exhausted and had a fever. I can't leave her here to die. It's going to snow in the mountains.* He dozed. *My children could ride with Charlotte. Yes, they could ride with Charlotte. No her wagon's full. I know, Thomas, yes,*

Thomas could drive our ox team. I can't leave her. I know she's alive. She has to be. I'll find her.

Streaks of lavender and pink painted the early morning sky as George leaned into the rear of their wagon.

I know it's here somewhere. He pawed through the piles. Their belongings had become disheveled in Elizabeth's absence and it had become increasingly difficult to find things. "Just need that other bag of gunpowder we bought in St. Louis," he muttered as he adjusted his stance to lean farther into the cavern. "There," he grabbed a dark gray stone. "And, I think I'll take that flint too." He scoured the wagon for other things he could use, added some dried antelope meat to the brown biscuits, and threw in a canteen. He rolled a quilt into a tight cylinder and cinched it with a rope. *That should do me fine.* He examined the collection of what frontiersmen call "possibles."

"Father," He felt a tug on his pant leg.

"Did you find Mum?" Desdemona looked up with frightened eyes. Still in her nightclothes, she had walked barefoot from Charlotte's wagon to find her Father.

"No, dear, we didn't." He picked her up. "But I'll find her." His voice was gentle and firm.

"But, Aunt Charlotte says we're leaving today. Is it true?"

"Yes, princess, today you leave for the Great Salt Lake."

"Can I ride on the perch?" She laid her head on his shoulder and he kissed her cheek. Her soft, curly hair intermingled with the course hairs of his beard.

"You can't, princess. You just can't." She saw the tears in her Father's eyes and hugged him.

"But, Father..." she pleaded, "I have to be with you. You're my Father, and Mum..." Her lip started to quiver and she tried not to cry.

"I know princess, I know." He was still holding Desdemona, his eyes shut tight, when Milo Andrus rode up.

"George," his voice cracked. "I'm so sorry. You know we have no choice but to go on. I understand how hard this is…" He glanced at the pile of goods at George's feet.

"What's this?" he asked, knowing the answer. "Planning to stay awhile are you?" Milo had felt compelled to talk to George and now he knew why.

George lifted his daughter into the back of the wagon and patted her head.

"I've got to find her!"

"You think you can do what fifty men couldn't do?"

"She's alive, I know she is."

"I realize this is hard to accept, but you've got to be reasonable. The footprints to the river…you said yourself that she can't swim. We've scoured every inch of brush."

"I know all that with my head, but…"

"Your children need you more than ever now. The last part of the trip is the hardest. We've got two mountain passes and…"

"Thomas can drive our team."

"No!" Milo shouted. Then, lowering his voice, tried to reason with him. "No, George, he can't. He's just a boy and it takes a man to handle those oxen. Besides, you won't survive. What if you find her? How do you get her to Fort Bridger?"

Milo stared at the ground and stated quietly, yet firmly, "You've got to come along. There's nothing more you can do here." He put his hands on George's shoulders, squarely facing him. "Elizabeth, God rest her soul, is with her Maker and I believe she would want you to take your children to Salt Lake. It was her dream."

"I know." George's response was barely audible. They hugged, strong arms reaching around each other with solid pats of reassurance.

As Milo mounted his horse, George knew what he had to do. He looked in on Desdemona. "It'll be all right," he said softly as he tucked the covers under her chin in the cool morning air.

He needed to be alone. He walked towards the tall cottonwoods. If only he could think of what to do. His mind was spinning, frantically searching for an answer. He dropped to one knee and the well of tears that he had held back for these many hours spilled over. *If only I had...where are you Betsy...where are you...God, help me...* His thoughts and tears churned together as he prayed. Gradually, calm permeated his soul and he was at peace.

His gait was slow and determined as he approached the wagon where his precious children lay sleeping. He gathered them to him and they knelt in a small circle next to their wagon.

"Father, please take care of our Mum," George's hoarse whisper touched his children. Desdemona cried and Mary put her arm around her. "Help her find her way," he prayed. "Help me to know what I should do, for I know not." His prayer continued. "We thank thee for our mother and ask for thy protecting hand to be over her." He took a deep breath and waited. "And, bless these children who are gathered here," his voice dropped. "And, bless me, as their Father, that I might have the strength to continue on."

He held his girls for a long time, stroking their hair as their sobs tugged at his broken heart.

George gave his son a long hug. "It will be all right, Thomas. Come along." Thomas followed his Father to the back of the wagon where frantically he dug through their belongings again. "Where's my tube cutter? I know it's here somewhere," he muttered under his breath. "Son, have you seen it since we used it at Independence Rock?"

"No, but I know Mum kept important things in the brown wicker box with the lid. I think it's on my side, I'll get it." He lifted himself into the wagon and crawled over bedding, food supplies and trunks until he found it. He opened the lid and there among dried wildflowers, smooth shiny rocks, and spools of thread was the tool they needed.

"We'll be back shortly." He told his daughters. They found the large boulder that George remembered from the previous day's searching. George's fine hand from years of lamp making aided him in engraving:

"Elizabeth Fox–lost Oct 10-1855-G S L"

The very act of etching the message lifted them. Perhaps it would help some traveler to find their mum and bring her on to the Great Salt Lake. As they turned to their chores of breaking camp and hitching up their oxen they were ready to move on. They longed for their mother, prayed constantly for her return and were comforted. The Rock of Salvation brought peace to their souls and the rock beside the trail brought hope to their hearts.

Chapter Nine

On to Fort Bridger

"Haw," George yelled as he walked to the left of the ox team. Clem, the lead ox on the right, was resistant to going across Black's Fork Creek for the third time. In the beast's mind he knew it was dry to the right and he pulled that way with all his oxen might.

Thomas whacked the big gray neck and joined in the "Hawing" as the ox hauled his weight away from his yoked partner.

"Come on Clem, move your big self over!" Thomas demanded as if he were David commanding Goliath, self-assured that the mammoth animal would respond to his direction.

"Haw, haw!" They were both yelling now. The ox was determined. The possibility of cramping the wagon was dangerously near. Another whack on the neck.

Desdemona and Mary gripped the sides of the wagon so hard their knuckles turned white. Teetering on two wheels for several seconds before the errant ox turned towards his master, the wagon thudded against the rocks when it fell onto four wheels with a splash. Elbows and knees askew, the girls bumped heads as they were thrown together like tumbleweeds.

"Whew! That was a close one!" George wiped his brow with the back of his hand as he stood knee deep in the ice cold water. The tipping of a wagon in a stream, although not always disastrous, could break the axle causing days of delay and, at the very least, drench the contents.

George peered into the wagon. "Are you all right, daughters?" They were rubbing their heads.

"Yes, Father," they replied together. They looked at each other and giggled.

The grass was green and dense where they camped on the flats above the creek not far from Fort Bridger.[10] Wind carved sculptures could be seen on the clay bluffs in the distance. With a bit of imagination the stone shapes seemed to take on life's images—tall English gentlemen, women in curtsy, children in a row.

"Thomas, see if you can angle a fish out of this stream." George pointed downriver where the stream had a deep eddy. "Girls, lets set up camp. You'll need to straighten up the wagon before sundown. That ol' Clem made quite a jumble of it."

He laughed at his own joke and the girls smiled politely. It had been three days since they left the east bank of the Green River. George tried to fill the void in their lives by teasing them and being unduly cheerful but his eyes betrayed his smile. They set up camp and built a fire on an already darkened circle of ashes.

"Look at this." Thomas proudly held up three mountain spotted trout. "This is the best fishing hole we've come across. We could go again at sunup and catch some for breakfast, tomorrow."

"Maybe. Looks like a real good supper to me." George took the trout from Thomas and laid them on the flat cooking iron affixed over the fire.

Won't this be a tasty supper, Betsy? His mind spoke to her constantly. *'Course, not as good as your antelope stew.* The loud crackle of the fire brought him back to reality.

"My girls, after this fine supper Thomas provided us, we'll need to hurry and straighten the wagon. Those dark clouds look threatening."

"It's going to rain." Mary twisted her hair around her finger. "It's going to rain on our Mum," she said sadly.

"I know you miss your Mum. We all do. But, we need to have faith, daughter." He hugged her. "She'll get out of the rain. She could stand under the trees. She could crawl into a cave. She could…" He couldn't imagine his Elizabeth, alone, doing the things he described. He choked up, held her hands and looked in her eyes. "I know she's alive, Mary. Someone will find her, I'm sure of it."

"Really, Father, really?"

"Yes, and tomorrow we're going south to Fort Bridger. Captain Andrus and I will meet with Lewis Robison, the trading post manager."

"Will you tell him about Mum?" Her eyes were dry now.

"Of course, m'dear." He put his arm around her shoulder and tugged her close to his side with a squeeze. "Of course. We'll have every mountaineer this side of the Mississippi looking out for her."

A crash of thunder made them all jump. They huddled together in their wagon and bedded down for the night. The wolf howls rode the wind as it slapped against their canvas cover and the rains poured.

"I hate wolfs." Desdemona shivered and ducked under her quilt. Mary pulled her quilt tightly under her chin and Thomas turned on his side to face his Father. The children woke often, anxious for a new day, a day that could help someone find their mother.

"There it is." Thomas pointed to the high picket fence surrounding Fort Bridger. They camped about a mile from the Fort where the grass was tall and lush. Fresh ice cold water from Rushing Creeks flowed in rivulets through the verdant valley. The distant Bear River Mountains, mottled in shades of purple and gray, towered majestically, snowcaps still in place from the winter of 1854, whitened by a layer of new snow received just days before.

"Take care of your sisters," George said sternly. "And no teasing!" His last words of instructions were surely to be disobeyed.

"Who me? Tease my sisters? Never." Thomas spoke loudly enough so his Father would hear. George and Milo headed for the trading post.

"Lewis! So good to see you." Milo grabbed his hand with both of his and shook heartily. "It's been a long time since Winter Quarters."

"That it has." Lewis Robison thought of how different his life was now as the newly appointed Mormon leader over Fort Bridger. The Mormon Church had recently purchased the famous trading post from mountain men Jim Bridger and Louis Vasquez.

"This is George Fox, one of our captains."

"Good to meet you, George." They shook hands and walked toward the trading lodge. The inner yard of the fort was about eighty feet long and forty feet wide with a couple of tepees by the log gate.

"So, you finally made it west. Last I heard you were outfitting the wagon trains in Kansas." Milo nodded as they stepped onto the porch of the trading lodge. Lewis motioned to the weathered wooden benches and they sat.

"The brethren asked me to bring this one all the way and it's been a good trip, except…"

Lewis leaned forward, elbows on knees, and raised his eyebrows in expectation.

"George's wife disappeared while we were camped on the east side of the Green River 'bout seven miles south of the ferry crossing. We spent two days searching but all we found was a set of her footprints near the river."

"Sorry to hear that," Lewis' sober expression said more than his words. "It's a dangerous river, but, sounds like you were considerable north of the Green River Suck where the current will suck you under before you can think." He sat up straight and folded his arms as he concentrated on the possibilities.

"One good thing," he said in a low voice. "We just signed a peace treaty with Washakie, Chief of the Shoshone Indians and their war with the Utes is over so they're not roaming the plains looking for trouble. And, supply trains going east trade here. I can mention to keep an eye out for her."

"I etched a message on a large rock by the trail. Hopefully someone will see it."

Lewis stared at the ground and shook his head. "It's a hardship. I am sorry."

"Thank you. I will be staying at the Franklin Richards' home in Salt Lake." He dug in his pocket and extracted a small piece of paper with large writing on it. "I wrote my name there for you and where I'll be staying. If you hear anything…"

"I'll be glad to help you in any way possible."

"Thank you for whatever you can do." George extended his hand again.

"Yes, thank you," Milo joined in.

"Whatever I can do…" Lewis accompanied them to the gate and watched George as he walked away. He wished he could do more.

Poor man. I'd hate to be in his shoes. He mulled over the possibilities. *It's been five days already and she doesn't have food, she does have water though. The nights are still above freezing, barely. Maybe, just maybe she can survive a few more days.*

He stepped up on to the porch, took off his hat, and bowed his head. *God help her.* He prayed silently. *It will take a miracle for her to be found, and to be found alive, that would be a mighty miracle.*

Chapter Ten

Forward to Zion

Remember Him (9)

T he trails to the Great Salt Lake had an occasional carved
sign and wagon ruts to mark the way. Splintered wheels,
abandoned wagons, empty barrels, and animal carcasses revealed
the struggles of previous travelers.

On the 14th of October, the Andrus Company set out on the
most difficult and last leg of their journey to the Great Salt Lake,
a trek of 113 miles. They crossed rock bedded creeks with frozen
chunks of floating ice and zigzagged up and down steep hills.
They passed by Red Mineral Spring where the water was an

unusual rusty color and smelled like rotten eggs. Mary and Desdemona huddled in the wagon for warmth as they ascended to the Bear River where the snow was packed and dirty at 7,000 feet. Finally, next to a small creek near Cache Cave, they set up camp.

Mary bent over to pick up one more twig for the fire when she saw them–three Indians galloping into camp at full speed. She gasped, dropped the wood, and ran for the wagon.

"Father, did you see them?" she yelled. "Indians. Over there." She pointed across the open space surrounded by wagons.

"What?" Desdemona poked her head out of the back of the wagon.

"Get in the wagon, Mary, and stay with your sister." He lifted her on to the perch. "I'm going to help Captain Andrus." He grabbed his rifle, glanced at the stewpot hanging over the fire, and headed off.

The camp looked deserted except for the men standing by their respective wagons, sentinels for their families. It was mostly quiet, women and children tucked away under their canvas covers, all eyes glued on the wagon master and visitors. As George walked up he could hear Milo.

Milo pointed to his chest then extended his hand. "Captain Andrus!" He enunciated loudly. He smiled broadly and repeated his signs of introduction.

The braves slid from their ponies creating a cloud of dust when their moccasins hit the ground. They stood with feet spread and arms folded across their chests. Their faces were sober. Dark eyes focused on Captain Andrus.

Are more hiding somewhere? Are these Shoshone? He looked the Indian directly in the eyes, not flinching. *Lewis said they're at peace now.* After what seemed like hours, the tension broke.

The tallest Indian stepped forward. "Howdeedo!" He pumped Milo's arm vigorously. "Howdeedo." He grinned, exposing yellowed teeth and black holes where teeth should have been. The other two Indians took turns in the same manner.

George joined them and they said their "Howdeedos" again and again as they shook hands. They stepped back, rubbed their bellies and smiled broadly bobbing their heads with feathers floating on their stringy, black hair.

"Food? Yes!" Milo nodded his head up and down, making sure they understood. Lewis had told them what to do if Indians came to their camp.

"They can have our soup," George offered. "We haven't eaten yet. There's plenty."

Milo motioned for them to follow George. They walked proudly, leading their ponies and speaking in a fast, guttural tongue. He poured soup into tin cups for them and watched as they gulped it down. He could see his daughters' eyes peeking from the wagon rim.

"Green River," he said, hoping they understood some English. "Squaw lost."

They nodded their heads in agreement. The leader rubbed his belly and held his cup out. George filled their cups.

"Squaw lost. Green River. You see?" He touched his eyes and held up his hand.

"Shoshone…Two Feathers…Bridger." The Indian tapped his chest then pointed to the south east and repeated, "Go Bridger. Two Feathers see Chief Washakie." George and Milo exchanged looks. George filled their cups once more and they left as quickly as they had come.

The girls climbed out of the wagon. "Father, do they know any words besides 'howdeedo?'" Desdemona giggled at Mary's silly question.

"I suppose they do...I hope they do," George rubbed the back of his neck, "but, that's the word they say the most."

"I hope so too. Maybe." Milo took off his hat and slapped it against his thigh creating a dusty cloud. "Thanks, George. I..." He was at a loss for words.

George clapped him on the shoulder.

"I know."

Thomas ran up yelling. "What did they say? Were they friendly? Where are they from?"

"I'll tell you later, son. I need to get to the camp counsel meeting. Did you get the oxen bedded down?"

"Yes, but I missed all the action." His complaint was ignored.

"You can take your sisters over to Cache Cave. It's that way," he pointed, "just a little over the hill. Return before dark."

"Please, Thomas, please." Desdemona and Mary pleaded in unison.

Thomas heaved a sigh, "I suppose I could take you...but, it will cost you...an extra biscuit in the morning, just for me," he teased.

They squinted as they entered the cavern, adjusting their eyes to the dim cave. Birds' nests sat on every rocky crag and the dirt floor was crawling with bugs.

"This is amazing. Smelly," she wrinkled her nose, "but, amazing." Mary reached up and touched the ceiling. Dirt fell and she brushed it off her shoulder. "How far do you think it goes?"

"I don't know, but come over here." Desdemona skipped to the side of the cave. "An egg." She held it up, rolling it between her fingers. "Should I keep it?"

"No!" Thomas and Mary agreed.

"Come on, Des," Thomas was the only family member that took the liberty of shortening her name. "Let's go in!" Mary hung on Thomas's arm and Desdemona held onto Mary's skirt as they crept into the darkness. Fluttering wings and bird chirps penetrated the silence. They could hear their own breathing in the cool, damp darkness. Desdemona looked behind her and felt relieved to see light filtering in at the mouth of the cave.

"Oh!" Thomas jumped as a bird flew past them. They nearly toppled over. "I think...this...is as far as I want to go."

They laughed as they told their Father of their fearless exploration. George laughed too, but his mind was on the Indians. *Will they find her? Did they understand me?*

The next day the girls teased Thomas about his bird ducking. They were on the trail shortly after sunup. The morning was chilly and cloudy. They traveled along a mountain stream into Echo Canyon, a narrow valley with hills on each side rising straight up for almost a thousand feet.

At noon meal Desdemona looked up from her plate of beans, "I thought the cave was the best thing we would ever see, but...have you tried singing out there, Mary?"

"Out where?"

"Just over there by those trees, if you sing toward that cliff, your song will come back to you, only, prettier than the first time, then it will come back to you again and again."

Desdemona loved Echo Canyon. "I think I shall sing for two days, which will really be like singing for four because of the echo." She swung her legs over the log and jumped up onto it. She sang "Tonight we'll dance by the light of the moon, to the fiddler's best and only tune." She stopped, and they all listened to the reply. They laughed with their own laughter.

For two days the echo of clattering wagons, clinking cowbells, cracking whips, and pioneer chatter was drowned out by the braying and lowing of animals repeatedly answering their own echoes. The noise was deafening. The exit from Echo Canyon bore a new respect for silence. The trail led over the rugged mountainous terrain of Main Canyon and up Hogsback Summit. Wagons and oxen were taxed to their limits. Autumn thundershowers drenched their camp creating such mire that the children had to push on the turning wheels to help the wagons through the mud.

From the top of Hogsback they could see mountains towering in every direction, a spectacular but disheartening view. They zigzagged to the bottom of the ravine into Dixie Hollow where they stopped and camped. Cold, wet and exhausted they ate, prayed and slept. *(Remember Him–9)*

They woke up to a heavy frost covering the fall leaves with a crystal blanket. The Aspens still had some yellow leaves hanging from dark twigs and the spruce trees had a sprinkling of frost that sparkled in the sunshine.

After breakfast they gathered for Sunday prayers and sermons. Captain Andrus spoke first. "Brethren, we must be grateful for this trail, broken for us almost ten years ago. Brigham Young came through this very valley, sick with yellow fever. His faith sustained him and all that were with him. Our faith must sustain us. The hardest part of our trip is made easier by taking a shortcut through Parley's Pass. That will save us four days of climbing mountains. They broke the road for us. They toiled and labored and we're grateful…, grateful that a loving Heavenly Father guided them and that He guides us now. Remember those who have sacrificed for you. And remember the supreme sacrifice of the Savior. Remember Him and his great love for you."

Thomas sniffed and bowed his head. *I miss Mum so much. I can't let my sisters down. I've got to be strong like my Father. Please bless my Mum, and my Father—to stay strong.*

Captain Andrus continued, "Many of you have lost loved ones on this trek or on other treks. God be with you and with your loved ones." He paused. "Be grateful for each other."

George put his arm around Mary.

I'm so glad I have Aunt Charlotte to help me. Mary was truly grateful. *She listens to me anytime. I know how busy she is being a nurse to Sister Snow and her family, but I thank you for her and for my Mum. Can you help the Indians find my Mum? Thank you Lord. Amen.*

Mary wiped her eyes and squeezed Desdemona's hand.

It's cold outside. Mum is cold. Please, God, take care of her. Don't let her be cold. You can bring her back to us, can't you? Angels could save her. Could you send your angels? Desdemona thought of her mother everyday, talking to her in her mind, praying for her.

The meeting closed with Sister Andrus singing a poem she had put to music. The melodic message resounded against the mountains.

Remember Him, Remember Him,
Oh My Savior, give me blessings I can share,
Warm my heart and bring me to your loving care,
Savior, I know you're there.

The Fox family spent the rest of the day exploring the mountainside. William and Jeremiah shot a couple of deer and shared the venison with the camp. The trek from here was treacherous and they were prepared.

The days blurred together as they made slow progress through the mountains. The creeks crisscrossed. In the valleys the willows grew like weeds. They were so thick and tangled. The Wasatch Mountains, beautiful with trees of forest green, red, gold and burnt umber, seemed endless. They climbed to the top of one peak, only to find another higher one on the other side. Finally, they ascended to the top of their last hill.

The view was spectacular. Looking into the orange sunset, the deep purple, snow-capped Oquirrh Mountains stretched north and south meeting the Wasatch Mountains in a notch at the south-ernmost point. Below the Oquirrhs, the aqua blue oval of Salt Lake shimmered. The wide flat valley looked like spun gold with spots on it. Surrounding the valley on the south and east were the Wasatch Mountains, sage green, gray, and purple with splotches of fall colors.

"Magnificent, there's no other word for it, magnificent." George and his children stood in awe.

"We'll be there tomorrow."

Chapter Eleven

Great Salt Lake

Little Boy's Eyes (10) followed by **Tiny Hands and Faces (11)**

The Andrus wagon train entered Salt Lake Valley on the evening of October 24, 1855. A small brass band played and residents of the city clapped and called out names of loved ones. Reunions were sweet with hugs and tears of joy.

"Charlotte Fox Richards," someone called. "Sister Charlotte Richards." Charlotte stopped her team, shocked to hear her name.

"Are you Charlotte Richards?" an elderly white haired man asked.

"Yes, I am."

She guided the team to the side of the street.

"I'm Samuel Tweed, a friend of your husband's. He wrote me six months ago and asked me to take you to the home he has for you. You must be weary."

"I thank you kindly, Brother Tweed. Franklin told me I would have a place to stay, but I didn't know…"

"And your brother's family? Will they be coming too? Franklin mentioned them as well."

"Yes, they're a few wagons back."

"If you wait here for them, I'll go get my carriage and you can follow me. It's a few miles from here." He politely tipped his hat. Charlotte nodded trying to control her impulse to jump down and give the stranger a huge hug.

Franklin's house was a welcome refuge for the weary travelers. It had been six months since they left their home in Birmingham. The four-room adobe house with its huge dooryard dotted with fruit trees dwarfed the wagons. *(Little Boy's Eyes–10)*

Samuel held the door open and Charlotte went in first. Modestly furnished, but clean, the home was accepted with deepest gratitude.

"Thank you," she shook his hand, "thank you."

"You are very welcome, my dear. I have a letter for you somewhere in here." He fumbled in his inside coat pocket, pulled out several papers and stuffed them back in. "Maybe…," he reached deep into his pants pocket, pulled out a crumpled envelope and handed it to her.

"I must be going. My wife will wonder where I am. She'll be bringing some foodstuffs for you in the morning. The best to you." He tipped his hat and opened the door. They followed him to the gate and waved as he rode away, then stood there in the moonlight until his carriage disappeared.

"He's a nice man. Will he come back to visit us?" Desdemona asked.

"I think so." Charlotte smiled. "We better get busy. It's freezing out here."

They unloaded their wagons sparingly. Charlotte brought in a few clothes and a quilt, the children brought their bedding, and George brought the rocking chair and scriptures.

"Thomas, get some logs from the woodpile behind the house and bring my ax."

"Mary, you and your sister lay out the bedding here and I'll go cut some kindling for a fire."

The fire warmed the house and their spirits as the flames cast their shadows on the walls.

"Father, will Mum find us here?"

"I'll make sure she can find us. Now, let's kneel for prayer. We've got much to be thankful for."

After prayer, Charlotte retired to her bedchamber. Thomas and Mary wrapped up in their quilts and stretched out on the floor. George began reading the scriptures to them as he rocked Desdemona. When she fell asleep he kissed her forehead and laid her on her makeshift bed. He continued reading until he nodded off.

Then he saw her, standing before him, in a flowing white dress. Beautiful. Hair curling about her shoulders, her face aglow, she smiled that familiar, lovely smile. She bent over Thomas and tenderly kissed his forehead. Then, kneeling by Mary, she held her daughter's hand, pressed it to her face, and kissed it. She sat by Desdemona for a long time caressing her hair and gently kissing her cheeks. She floated toward him as if on a cloud. He could feel her hands on his face, her eyes smiling. Her warmth seemed to envelop him.

He reached for her. Following her to the doorway, he felt a tug on his pant leg. Desdemona held up her arms and he lifted her up. He looked and Elizabeth was gone. Softly, she left as she had come, in a breath. His cheeks were wet as he held his daughter in his arms and rocked her back to sleep.

On his first day in Salt Lake, George walked to the Council House on the corner of South Temple and Main to inquire about his wife. He was referred to Brother Whetstone, the clerk who tracked the comings and goings of emigrant trains, missionaries and dignitaries. George related the details of Elizabeth's disappearance and informed him of where he was staying.

Every day George visited the clerk and asked the same question.

"Any word on m'wife, Elizabeth?"

"No, Brother Fox." The silver-haired clerk was so accustomed to his query that he would sadly start the negative nodding even before George asked the question.

"You know where I will be if you hear anything?"

"Yes, George, I'll find you, if you don't find me first." He looked over the glasses balancing on the tip of his nose.

The first few weeks were full of new experiences for everyone. Charlotte cooked and cleaned and wrote letters to her husband in England. George reorganized all of their belongings, bringing into the house their foodstuffs, clothing and perishables and leaving the tools in the wagon. *(Tiny Hands and Faces–11)*

Thomas, Mary and Desdemona attended the one room schoolhouse about a mile from their house. The school was for all grades with one schoolmaster. Books were scarce but discipline was abundant. Desdemona was usually the first to arrive home.

"How did you like school today?" Charlotte wiped her hands on her apron as she turned to Desdemona.[11]

"It's all right. I like Violet. She's a nice girl, but…"

"But, what?" Charlotte looked puzzled. She knew the school courses of reading, writing, arithmetic and history would not prove difficult for Desdemona, and, she was comfortably schooled in the social graces.

"Thomas just made fools of us all. He teased the girls and got the other boys to do it too. They took our books and made fun of all the girls. He's such a big bully sometimes. I can't stand boys!"

"Hmmmm," she sighed as she rested one hand on her hip and, with the other, wiped the flour off her nose.

"It can be annoying, but, endearing too. In fact, I think that is what attracted me to my dear husband." Charlotte blushed. "He is quite the tease. Bless his good soul; he has a joyous temperament in him that keeps me quite intrigued." Fond thoughts of her Franklin, still in England, were quickly abated with the pressing task at hand.

"Come, help me with these biscuits."

They were busily cutting the dough into small squares when George walked in. His demeanor told all.

"Not a word again today." He hung his hat on the peg by the kitchen door.

"I'm so sorry." Charlotte sensed his daily disappointment but she didn't know what else to say to her brother. Common sense told her that his dear Elizabeth was in Heaven and she would want George to go on with his life as best he could.

"George, I am so sorry." She began again. "I miss her too. And the children." She looked over at Desdemona busily patting the dough into brown heaps. Her eyes filled. "My heart aches for them."

George slumped in the chair, "The children, ah, yes. How tender they are and how rough a man I am. Just can't do it, just ca…," his voice caught.

Desdemona ran over and jumped onto her Father's lap giving him a round-the-neck hug.

"It's all right, Father. Jesus will take care of Mum. I know he will." She snuggled closer and the three of them hugged.

Mary rushed in and stopped.

"Father, are you well?"

"I'm fine, daughter." He regained his composure quickly. Desdemona hopped down. Charlotte wiped her eyes with the tip of her apron.

"Those biscuits surely need our attention," she muttered as they returned to their task.

"Father, there's a social Friday next," Mary began enthusiastically. "*Everyone* is going." She put extra emphasis on the "everyone," then continued her petition.

"Can we go? Can we? Thomas said he wanted to go. He told me this afternoon."

George shook his head with the first breath of the word "social." That was the last thing he wanted to attend.

"No," he exhaled the word. "No, I don't think so."

"But everyone is going, Father. It's what everyone does here."

"No. Thomas never finished his dancin' lessons with your Mum." He caught his breath. "And you're just a bit of a young lady. No, we shan't be going to any…"

"Well, now George," Charlotte interrupted. "Maybe it's not such a bad idea. I understand from the sisters at the Mercantile that the Harvest Social is one of the best of the year. It celebrates the end of the harvest, slim as it has been this year, and we give thanks for what God has provided."[12] She thought of the rationing the saints were asked to do to preserve enough grain for the incoming emigrants.

"It might be just the thing for the children. It's not like *you* have to dance. Most everyone takes their families and blankets for the children so they can sleep when the mood strikes them." Charlotte made a strong case for her niece and nephew and, she felt, for her brother George, as well.

"My friend, Orson, says we will have our first square dance lesson at school tomorrow. So, I'll be ready." Thomas brought in a load of freshly chopped kindling and dropped it into the woodbox. He hung his hat on the peg next to his Father's.

"I'm going to be a great step dancer just like you, Father." He leaned on the table and grinned.

The Harvest Social was held in the basement level of the Social Hall, a two-story building made of red sandstone that was completed in 1852. Like bees in a beehive the citizens of Salt Lake swarmed into the hall. Mary and Thomas hurried down the stairs.

"Come on, Father." Thomas impatiently beckoned. "We'll be late." George and Charlotte followed with Desdemona holding her aunt's hand.

"I don't know about this, Charlotte. I understand the children's need for recreation but I'm not ready for…"

"I realize that George, I know you wait for Elizabeth and I wait for Franklin, but it is good to see the merriment, don't you agree?"

Suddenly Mary stopped. The scene before her was breathtaking. Little children sat on colorful quilts lining the sides of the hall. They played cat's-in-the-cradle and peas porridge hot, laughing and talking, pulling on their mama's skirts. Ladies, dressed in their finery, such as they had, chatted and smiled, nodding their heads, eyeing their husbands and each other. The men, most jovial, greeted one another with handshakes and claps on the back. A bevy of fiddlers tuned their violins slowly drawing their bows across the strings while the guitar players plunked at the fifth frets. Then a hush.

A prayer of thanksgiving was met with bowed heads followed by an "Amen" that rang though the hall.

George, tall and stately, stood apart from the group as he held Desdemona's hand. They watched, fascinated. The men promenaded their partners creating patterns of circles and squares to the lively music. The ladies curtsied and pointed their toes. The men bowed and smashed their heels against the floor. They all clapped their hands to the enticing rhythms. Surrounding the dancers small groups of onlookers chatted politely. Mothers checked their sleeping children and tucked the covers under their chins.

At last George tucked Desdemona into her mother's quilt. He kissed her forehead, a private message that she was his princess and she should go to sleep.

Memories flooded his mind. *I miss you, Betsy, I truly do.* He felt the sharp pain in the center of his chest again. It was not as sharp as the knife-like pains of those first few futile days of searching, but still it returned, more severely when his thoughts were heavy.

His eyes were blind as he looked into the swirl of skirts. *I'll wait for you! I will!* He longed to hold her, to hear her soft laughter and to look into her eyes. He needed her unwavering faith. He remembered her words as she stood in the dooryard of their modest cottage in Birmingham chiding him for being discouraged with the small savings they had put away for emigrating.

Now, George the Lord doesn't expect anything from us we can't manage. We'll be going to Zion. That we will. We will be going. Her words rang in his mind.

You were right, Betsy. We are here. In Zion. Where are you? He offered the prayer that he always carried in his heart.

Father, keep her in thy hand. Guide someone to find her,
Father. Protect her…

Chapter Twelve

Lost

The frost melted in the midday sun. Patiently waiting for their prey, two buzzards circled above the rocky rim. The Green River, with its deep, green pools, swiftly carried brown and yellow cottonwood leaves in swirls of frothy bubbles through the rocky hills of Wyoming

She lay there beneath the flat rock shelf, face down. Limp, wet, cold. Her right leg was drawn up to her chest. Her right arm, crisscrossed with scabs, dried blood and oozing wounds, was draped across her knee. Her long hair sprawled across her back. Tangled with bits of leaves and grass, matted and dirty, it provided an ideal home for crawling insects. A mosquito found its harvest on her cheek. Instinctively she brushed it away. Her lips parted, her tongue searched for moisture. Her eyes opened as narrow slits and then quickly closed, opened again, this time a little wider, but still not seeing, closed once more. Her brow wrinkled and her eyebrows knit as she concentrated on opening her eyes.

"Aaaaahgh!" She straightened her cramped leg.

Rolling onto her back, she squinted at the glaring sun and raised her arms instinctively to shield her eyes. *Where...where am I?* Her mind wandered, searching for answers.

She tried to collect her thoughts. Echoes of her name resounded in her memory. E-liiiz-a-beth...E-liiiz-a-beth. She vaguely remembered footsteps and shouting.

She groaned as she turned onto her side, her body ached and her head pounded. Her cracked lips and parched throat made it hard to swallow. Random thoughts passed through her mind, strung together like pearls on a string with knots between them.

I'm so tired... I need to get up... I can't... Sleep... I'll sleep... Who is calling me? I'm coming... Nooooo, I can't come... I'm sooooo weary... Sleep... I must sleep.

She lay still. Time was neither real nor important. Long tendrils of orange, pink, and purple now streaked across the once blue sky. She stirred, opened her eyes to this softer light, took a deep breath and listened. The rustling leaves, the buzzing flies, and the water—it was the sound of the splashing, bubbling water that brought her to her senses.

Elizabeth struggled to her feet, stood for a moment and staggered forward, her head reeled and blackness veiled her eyes.

"Ohhhhhhhh," she moaned as she crumbled to the ground. She lay quietly, giving her head time to clear. She pulled herself onto her hands and knees and inched herself up. Waiting, she stood statue-like and squinted to see the river below her.

Water, I'm so thirsty. I've got to have water.

Splotches of blood marked her trail as she picked her way between the sharp, wind-carved rocks. Propelled by the steep incline, she ran too fast, clumsily stumbled, and slid on the loose shale to the riverbank's packed sandy loam. It was soft and smooth to her injured feet. She stretched straight out on the bank, her chest and arms hanging over the water. Cupping her hands, she gulped the cold water until she could drink no more. Refreshed, she sat for a long time picking thorns from the festered sores on her hands.

Her brow furrowed as she searched her memory for an inkling of why she was here, alone. Haunting memories lingered. Again she heard someone calling her name. *Where is everyone?*

Her thoughts were muddled, but her instincts were clear. She had to survive. She shivered, rubbed her arms, and gazed across the river. Thick gray reeds grew together like rows of tall pipe organs with an occasional path that cut down to the water. She saw a berry patch with thorny, twisting branches and for the first time became aware of her hunger.

Elizabeth stood again, this time more easily, and meandered along the barren riverbank. It was dark when she reached a small grove of cottonwood trees. She leaned against a trunk and slid down into the bed of yellow and orange leaves. Ignoring her hunger, she welcomed sleep.

The morning frost covered her blanket of leaves. She could see her breath as she blew on her fingers. Rubbing her hands together, she tucked them between her thighs and hunched down tucking her nose in the front of her dress. Her breath warmed her. Her joints were stiff and she ached from the cold so she slapped her arms and shook her legs hoping for relief. At last, she knelt, calmly folded her arms, and bowed her head.

I am so cold, I need food, Please help me... Her prayer was answered.

She walked downstream for what seemed like hours before finding a wild berry patch like the one across the river. Ravenous, she picked the berries off the bushes and scoured the ground, stuffing them into her mouth as fast as she found them. The sun peeked from the clouds and warmed her. At sunset she returned to her refuge in the leaves.

Each day was like the day before except for a thundershower now and then. Always she prayed: for protection, for food, for warmth. The long walk to get food had become increasingly difficult as she weakened. The howling of the wolves seemed closer, and the buzzards still circled. But, each night she felt safe as she lay under the coverlet of leaves at the base of the cottonwood tree.

What was that? Her eyes flew open. She sat up. The frost covered leaves cascaded from her shoulders. She listened. A horse whinnied. Her eyes followed the sound, then, she saw them. Three mounted Indians at the top of the ridge exactly where she had been days before. Their horses pawed the rocks as the tall Indian in the middle pointed toward the river. His stringy black hair was adorned with hanging feathers. He gestured toward her as he spoke and the Indians beside him nodded their heads in agreement.

Oh, please, Lord, don't let them see me! Her heartbeat pounded in her ears. She held her breath. *Don't move.* She coached herself. Her back hurt. Her legs cramped. *Why are they still looking at me?* Her neck tightened, but she did not move.

The Indians scanned the horizon as they turned their horses slowly, much too slowly for Elizabeth. They galloped over the hill and out of sight. She stayed perfectly still until their clouds of dust settled. She took a deep breath and let it out slowly.

Tears flowed. *Thank you, Lord, thank you.* Warmth washed through her. She was calm. She was at peace.

Chapter Thirteen

The Other Side of the River

Camped on the banks of the Big Sandy Creek, Jedediah Sandene opened one eye. "Jumpin-jee-hosifats, we gotta get goin'," he said to himself. He sat up, yanked his leather boots on, and plopped on his coonskin hat. He'd hauled supplies from St. Louis to Sacramento and back for the last four years and he always followed the advice in the *Emigrants Guide to California*: "From the Big Sandy Creek to the Green River," it stated, "Recollect, do not attempt to cross during the day, for a distance of thirty-five miles there is not a drop of water."[13]

"Git up! What in tarnation do y'think we're gonna do? Nap all night long?" He rousted his men off their bedrolls with the tip of his boot. "We gotta git to the Green River by sunup and that's nigh on thirty-five miles, so's ya better jest git movin' right quick, by crackey. Thar ain't no time for no more nappin'!" He chucked his bedroll into the wagon.

"Sarah, give the men some of yer biscuits and coffee. Jerky's in the wagon box." Sarah, the only woman on the trek, rolled up her single braid and tucked it into her leather hat. Strands of graying hair escaped but at least it was out of her way.

The fringe on his buckskins bounced as he hitched up his horses. A short, compact man with a big voice and a full beard infested with beard-bugs, Jedediah scratched his chin almost as much as he talked.

"No time fer nothin', jest a movin'." His orders, sprinkled with warnings, motivated the men. Their afternoon naps were quickly abandoned and they were on the trail in the cool of the evening.

"Cold as blue blazes up here!" Jedediah spoke to no one in particular as he adjusted the reigns and pulled his buffalo robe closer. "October jest ain't a good time to come through this here high country. Jest a keep on movin thar, Buckeye." Jed spoke to the stallion like an old friend, "this here's our night ride and we got jest a little ways to go." He chuckled at his cleverness and clucked his tongue a couple of times. "I am getting a wore out m'self. My mouth's dry as a cotton ball in July." They traveled on in quiet, making good time, thirty-two miles in thirteen hours.

"Will ya look at that! Thar she is, all green and shinin' under the risin' sun. That thar river is a gift, pure and simple, a gift from the Maker." Jed continued his monologue, "I knows yer thirsty. Jest gotta keep a goin' thar, Buckeye. Up the road apiece I think. Yessiree, there's that boulder I always look fer sittin' right thar. Will ya looky thar, it's dun got some 'ritin' on it." He jabbed his elbow into his sister's side.

"Sarah! Kin you read that thar 'ritin' on that rock?"

"Wha…? Wha' rock? No, it's too dark fer me to see it, Jed. Sun's not up enough yet." She squinted.

"F-O-X," Jed said each letter. "Fawx," he sounded out the word. "It says somethin' Fox. Why'd a feller rite on a rock? Jest don't make no sense t' me." He shook his head, scratched his chin, and flicked the reigns.

"Thar ya be, I kin see it up ahead, the Mormon Ferry crossing. See that Buckeye, thar's yer waterin' hole. Guess 'n I better git my money out for the dadgum toll." He felt his money pouch at his waist, "yep, this'll take some timin' Buckeye, so's you kin rest a bit." They watered the horses and waited for each wagon to have its turn.

"Hey, Cecil, ketch this one in yer paw!" Jed chomped on the green apple picked fresh from the wild apple tree up the trail a bit. "Here ya go!" He threw one to his friend who was being ferried across the 250 foot span of water. The rafts, fitted with rudder and oars, took all eight wagons, one at a time.

Once across, they hitched up again and traveled south along the west side of the river about ten miles, looking for a place to camp for the noon meal.

"Thar's some trees fer us, Sarah, rite thar in that gully on the riverbank. Whoa thar, Buckeye!" Jed coached his horse to a stop and jumped down off the perch. The other wagons pulled up beside him.

"Git on down thar, men. Them horses are dry as a bone. Git a move on thar, Sarah." He motioned for her to help him unharness the horses. He slapped his horse on the hindquarter and the mares followed Buckeye to the water.

Jed was real proud of his spinster sister, plain-looking though she was. She could ride a horse, shoot a gun, wrestle a man down, and spit with the best of them. She was also a good cook, which was the main reason Jed brought her along.

"Hold it!" He held his arm out as a command for silence. He leaned forward; the horses lifted their heads, water dripping from their bridles and looked downriver. Everyone froze. Jed crept back to the wagon, set the harness down and picked up his rifle. Sarah followed close behind.

"Somethin's in that thar thicket," he whispered in a husky voice. He crouched down behind the corner of the wagon, and squinted, trying to detect what had caught his eye. Slowly, he raised the long Winchester to his shoulder in one smooth movement. "Steady, thar Jed," he said to himself.

Sarah, glued to him, strained to see. She had roamed the country enough to know that self-preservation depended on a quick decision and an accurate shot. Her hand reached for Jed's shoulder, instinctively. She ignored the mosquito on it.

Then, the bushes moved again. She heard the click of the hammer. The only thing left was to squeeze the trigger. "Steadyyyy, steadyyyy."

"No!" Sarah screamed, knocking the rifle barrel off target and Jed off balance. "Whet ja doin', thar Sarah. Dad gummitt. Are you plumb crazy?" Jed blustered after missing the shot.

"That's a woman down there, Jed!" Sarah could also yell with the best of them. "You can't shoot no woman!"

"Don't look like no woman t'me. What's a woman doin'out in these here…?"

Before he could finish Sarah barreled past him. She raced for the thicket, hurdled through the brush, and almost stumbled over Elizabeth hiding behind a berry bush.

Aghast at the sight of her, Sarah said quietly, "My, my, my. Aren't you a sight for sore eyes!"

Elizabeth's sunken cheeks and darkened eyes told the story of her suffering. Her hair was matted with dirt and dried leaves. Her dress was torn and her feet were bloodied.

It was all Sarah could do to keep from crying when she looked at her. "You poor thing! Whatever happened to you?" She took off her coat and wrapped it around her.

"Thank you." Elizabeth spoke but no sound came out.

"There, there," Sarah clucked as she knelt down and tenderly put her arms around the frail Elizabeth.

Suddenly all of the emotions Elizabeth held inside broke lose. She buried her face in the large woman's shoulder and cried until there were no more tears to cry.

"You'll be awright. You'll be jest fine," Sarah patted her. "You'll be jest fine, yes, you will. Jest fine." Her eyes welled. "There, there."

"Well I'll be…!" Jed let out a slow whistle. "You is a woman!" He shook his head in disbelief. "What in tarnation happened to ya? You look like you took a lickin'!"

Sarah shot him a look that would have killed a buffalo.

"Who are ya and whatcha doin' in these here parts all by yerself?"

Elizabeth took a deep breath. She didn't have many answers for him. She didn't know how she got there. She could only remember being alone in the cold and the pangs of hunger.

"My name," she stammered as she struggled to stand, "is Elizabeth." She regained enough of her composure to stay upright, leaning slightly on Sarah.

"I've come from Birmingham and I am on my way to the Great Salt Lake." How she knew that much she wasn't sure. She just knew it, like she knew her name.

"Hmph, aint that jest dandy!" Jed spit his tobacco in a wide arc past the bushes and scratched his chin. "You gotta ways to go. Where's yer kinfolk?"

"I...I don't know."

"Gess you kin hitch a ride t' Fort Bridger with me. Looks like ya need some doctorin't' me."

"How...can... I...thaaaank.." Her speech slurred as the color drained from her face. Sarah caught her on her way down.

"She's plumb passed out, Jed."

Jed scooped her up in his arms. "Whatcha all gawkin' at? "Can't ya see this here is a purebred lady? Be fixin' up a bed for her in m' wagon."

Chapter Fourteen

A Resting Place

Lewis stood at the open gate and looked out past the willow trees to a rise in the road where a cloud of dust predicted a wagon train about to arrive at Fort Bridger.

"Looks like another train arriving," he stated to himself.

My children will like that. Been a little dull around here lately, he thought, as he walked back to the trading post. *Better see how those boys are doin' stocking the shelves.*

Good thing the flour came in. We'll have plenty to last the winter. Got some potatoes too. The Indians surely do like potatoes. Maybe, just maybe, the peace treaty will hold this time.

His thoughts were those of a provider of goods, a storekeeper that could aid the emigrants and keep peace with the Shoshones. *They'll be visitin' as soon as the snow flies and I'll be ready to feed them.* He stepped into the room and absentmindedly pulled on his suspenders as he inspected their work.

"Papa, we're finished." John and Matthew stood proudly, thumbs under their suspenders, rocking back and forth from their toes to their heels.

"Can we go fishin' now? They're bitin' somethin' fierce."

Lewis slowly paraded by each shelf inspecting the neat stacks of boxes and bags. He hesitated by the flour barrel. Out of the corner of his eye he could see his boys squirm. He looked at them with a stern expression and said, "All right. You can go fishing; just bring some home this time!" He laughed, gave John a swat on the behind and out the door they went.

"Well, lookee thar, gotta couple of young 'uns here." Jedediah dodged them as they charged out the door. "We're lookin' fer Bridger," he stated flatly.

"Jim Bridger hasn't been here for over a year now. I'm Lewis Robison. Can I help you?" Lewis held out his hand as he responded. He was used to conversations beginning like this. Most of the traders didn't know the fort had been purchased by the Mormons and was under reconstruction.

"That so?" Jed shook hands looking him straight in the eyes. ("You kin measure a man if he looks y' squar'," he always said.) Lewis passed the test.

"I s'pose you'll do." Jed said under his breath. "Yer a-talkin' to Jedediah Sandene and this here's m'sister Sarah and m' wagon drivers, William, we call him Billy, and Amos." He spat on the floor, took his hat off, ran his hands around the fur forming it into shape, and slapped it back on his head.

"I gotta Mormon woman in m'wagon that needs some doctorin' real bad." His face was sober.

"Your wife?"

"Well, I'll be a wokeup grizzly bear, no I aint gotta wife!" He snickered. "But, I found this here Mormon woman…go git her." He motioned his men to the door with his head making the tail on his raccoon hat swing like a pendulum. "As I was sayin', been up by the Green River, now thar's a pretty un ain't it?" He paused, "and this woman popped up outta nowhere. Nearly shot her. If it weren't for Sarah's sharp eyes, I wouldda done jest that." He licked his lips and swallowed hard.

Sarah piped up, "Yep, I jest kept lookin' and a lookin' and I thought…that's a woman peekin' outta them bushes. So I jest shoved his barrel a bit." She reenacted the scene, smiling all the while. Her face wrinkled around her mouth and her hazel eyes twinkled. She loved being the hero.

Jed reached in the small leather bag hanging on a thong around his neck and pulled out a plug of tobacco and stuffed it in his cheek.

"Says her name is Elizabeth."

"Impossible."

"Nope. Ain't impossible, that's her name, sure as shootin'."

"Yep, that's her name all right. She told me right off," Sarah confirmed.

"Oh, I believe that's her name. I'm just amazed. Her husband… if she's the same Elizabeth, and I assume she is, he came in here a couple of weeks ago or so." He remembered it well for he thought the woman had little or no chance of survival and he had purposely avoided looking at George squarely, so as not to belie his thoughts.

"He was absolutely sure someone would find her. Told me he scratched her name into the big boulder next to the tra…"

"Hold it." Jed took a step closer. "You sayin', the boulder on the trail east of the Green, jest past the bend?"

"I'm not sure, I haven't seen it, I just heard about it. It had her name on it though, Elizabeth Fox."

"By durnd, that's the one." He slapped his breeches. "Remember Sarah, I read that name to ya right off'n that rock, F-O-X. Yep, that's the name, Fox." He grinned and scratched his chin.

"He left me a note of where he'd be staying." Lewis rustled through a drawer for the scrap of paper. "Here it is. 'Richards,' that's the name. Her husband, George, said he'd be staying with his sister in the Franklin D. Richards home when he reached Salt Lake."

"Well, I'll be durned, thar ya be. Guess'n' you kin get them two together." He leaned across the desk and planted his elbows as if his extra pair of eyes would help in deciphering the note.

"Maybe. It's late in the season, but there might be another wagon train through here."

"Well, there ya be," Jed swatted a mosquito off his wrist. "Dadgummed skeeters! Never seen 'em so thick 'ceptin' in this here territory."

Amos was breathing hard by the time he carried Elizabeth from the wagon, across the dooryard, up onto the wooden porch and through the door. Cradled, her arms were around his neck and her head rested on his shoulder. Her hair hung to her waist. Her rust colored dress was filthy and torn. Her feet and legs were swollen. Scabs that had formed on her wounds were cracked and oozed blood and puss. Her arms and face were streaked yellow and green from bruises still healing and covered with red welts where mosquitoes fed. Open sores festered around the thorns imbedded in the palms of her hands. The most heartbreaking of all was her face, gaunt and colorless, skeletal looking. It was particularly haunting because her green eyes burned brightly in stark contrast to her sickly appearance.

Lewis gasped at the sight of her. "Emily," he said quietly. "Emily, come here quick!" he yelled.

"What's the matter?" His wife came running but stopped short. "Oh, my heavens. Oh!" She gasped. Her eyes filled. "Oh my." She shook her head in disbelief. "I've never..."

"She ain't good," Sarah declared soberly.

"We'll put her in the boys' room," Lewis declared briskly, "Amos, you follow me. Emily, bring her a cup of barley soup off the cookstove," he directed. "Come along, Sarah." She looked at Jed and he nodded.

"Dunno why she's still alive. She musta froze herself come nighttimes." Sarah jabbered as Amos laid her on the cot. "She slept most the ride gettin' here. I tried to comb her hair. Didn't do much good though, She don't remember much. Jest her name, and that she's from Birmingham going to the Great Salt Lake. She kin smile though. Yep, she's got a beauty of a smile, her eyes light up like the fourth of July."

"Here dear, let me help you." Emily lifted Elizabeth to a half sitting position and held the cup for her.

"She et some biscuits and some hard tack today. Not much of a eater, the soup'll do her good."

"You've been so good to her, Sarah."

"Twernt nothin'...wouldda done it fer anybody." Sarah beamed.

Elizabeth reached for Sarah's hand and squeezed it. "I must thank you," she said softly. "You have been so kind, you and Jed."

"Sarah!" Jed yelled. "Sarah, we gotta git a move on."

He turned to Lewis. "I wanna be past three mile crik and the springs afore sundown. M'horses loves the bunchgrass in that clearing there between the criks. Ever been there?"

"Can't say I have."

"Too bad." He hollered, "Sarah!" Then, lowering his voice he asked, "how much do I owe ya? Got some flour, wagon grease and hard tack."

"It's all right. My pleasure to serve you." Lewis extended his hand. "You and your men grab a cup of soup before you leave. Cups are right there by the cook stove."

"Don't mind if I do. Hey, Amos, you and Will get yerselves some grub. Sure smells good." He motioned to the others, "you, too."

"Take care of yerself, Lizzy," Sarah gave her a long hug.

"I'll never forget you, Sarah," Elizabeth whispered.

Wiping her eyes with the back of her hand, Sarah walked briskly to the doorway. She heard Jed giving orders to his teamsters. She didn't stop for soup, but hastened to their wagon so Jed wouldn't see her crying. If there was one thing he couldn't tolerate it was a blubberin' woman.

"Sarah's gone to the wagon." Lewis slapped Jed on the shoulder.

"Guess we'll be a leavin'. Thanks for the grub and all."

"My pleasure. Have a safe journey." They shook hands heartily and Jed was off spewin' and spoutin' all the way to the wagons.

Bless them, Lord. Lewis prayed silently as he waved from the porch. *Keep them safe.*

"Lewis," Emily, came up behind him, put her arms around his waist and squeezed. "Quite the miracle," she said. She laid her head against his back.

"More than you know." He turned around and kissed her. For some reason he felt unusually romantic.

"How is she doing?"

"Better. She's sleeping now. What an ordeal! I can't even imagine. How long was she out there?"

"Close to two weeks, I think."

"Did she tell you anything?"

"She doesn't remember anything—only her first name. I'll tell her about her husband when she wakes up. You know the strangest thing just occurred to me," he paused, deep in thought. "I've been thinking about the boulder on the trail. They must have been camped on the east side of the river. Right?"

"I suppose. Is that where you approach the Green River if you're coming from Big Sandy?"

"Yes."

"And, so?"

"Jed said they'd already crossed on the ferry and were traveling down the west side of the river when they found her."

"So how did she get to the other side?"

"Maybe she swam. I don't know."

"I don't know, either, but let's go in. I'm sure hopin' those boys bring home some trout for dinner." She gave him another squeeze before going in.

Elizabeth slept soundly. For the first time in days she wasn't cold. She yawned and lazily stretched. *It's so nice to be warm!* She snuggled down under the patchwork quilt and pulled it over her head.

"How are you feeling?" Emily set a warm biscuit on the pine table by her cot.

"I'm fine," came out muffled as she emerged from her self-made cocoon. "I feel so much better." Elizabeth sat up, and grimaced as pain shot through her head. "Oooh," she squiggled back down. "I'll stay here for awhile."

"Probably a good idea. When you're ready, sit up slowly. We want to tend to your wounds today so I'll come back in a couple of hours."

I'm in Fort Bridger. I wonder how close that is to Salt Lake. I don't know what I would do if I did get there. I don't know anyone.

Emily heated water and poured it into a glass basin, tore bandages from some leftover muslin, found her finest needle, and some squares of lye soap.

"Ow!" Elizabeth flinched. "Sorry," she apologized to her nurse. Her muscles tensed as she held out her right thumb. Her forehead was beaded with sweat. She clenched her jaws and squeezed her eyes tightly preparing for the next jab. All day, dirt, rocks and debris had been literally scraped out of her wounds. Scrubbed scabs left her raw flesh dotted with beads of blood. Emily put this one off until last.

Red and swollen to twice its size she dug into a puss pocket that had formed around Elizabeth's thumbnail. Yellowish white liquid bubbled out relieving the pressure but not the soreness.

"We'll have to soak it and hope the infection drains. I can't find the thorn. I'll go get a clean basin of hot water." She wiped her hands on her apron as she left her patient.

Lewis walked in. He had been waiting for an opportunity to talk to Elizabeth. "So, how's our miracle woman today?" he teased.

"I am certainly cleaner," she answered pleasantly. "This is quite the nurse you're married to. In fact, you might call her Doc Robison."

He liked her sense of humor. "I'm Lewis Robison," he introduced himself. "I know we met yesterday but I wasn't sure if I told you my name."

"I guess you know I'm Elizabeth."

"I know your name is Elizabeth Fox."

"Fox? That's my last name?"

"Yes, your husband George came through here about two weeks ago. He wanted me to know where he would be staying in Salt Lake so you could find him."

"I have a husband…George? Yes…George." Teary eyed, she mulled it over. Was he tall, with brown hair? And a beard, a brown beard? Was he wearing a plaid shirt? And, did he have blue eyes with thick eyebrows?" Lewis nodded affirmatively with each question.

"As a matter of fact, he did. I don't remember the color of his eyes though." Lewis chuckled under his breath.

She smiled, "I remember." She had a faraway look in her eyes. *We were sweethearts…I remember…*

He told Elizabeth all he knew: the two-day search, the Andrus wagon train, and the footprints to the river. Then he stopped.

"You know, you were found on the west side of the river, but your camp was on the east side. Did you really swim across? No one's ever done that, at least that I know of."

"I can't swim," she said, searching her mind for clues. "I don't know. I can't remember. I know I'm afraid of water so I have never learned to swim."

"Hmmmm. Well, maybe it will come to you. Probably not important anyway. The important thing is that you're here, safe. And, as soon as you are well enough to travel, we'll find a wagon train to take you to Salt Lake."

Elizabeth did get stronger with time, sleep and nourishing food. The dark circles under her eyes vanished and color came back into her cheeks. Her wounds were healing but her memory was still missing big chunks. She could remember herself as a young girl, her mother and father, her courtship and marriage, but beyond that—nothing. She napped in the afternoons and helped Emily in the mornings with the cooking and cleaning.

It was early in the morning when three Shoshone Indians paraded in with chests puffed out, heads held high. A fat, weathered squaw trailed behind them pulling a miniature travois loaded with deer and elk hides. They piled the skins on the wooden floor.

"Trade, whiskey." The tallest Indian with the feathers woven in his hair stated his offer. "Me two feathers." He tapped his chest. "Trade, whiskey."

"No whiskey, whiskey all gone." Lewis shook his head.

"No whiskey?" He said something in his language sprinkled with "whiskey" to his cohorts. "No whiskey?" He wanted to make sure. Lewis shook his head, looking sad. "Potatoes?" The Indian asked.

"Yes, plenty of potatoes," Lewis nodded. The squaw smiled.

Wondering what the ruckus was, Elizabeth entered the room and hesitated.

She quietly walked over and gently stroked the plaid blanket wrapped about the squaw's shoulders. She ran her fingers along the hem, then up and down the folds. Impressions washed over her. Thoughts flooded her mind. She saw a gravesite under some trees. *He's still. A baby...my baby...so tiny.* She saw herself hand the baby to her husband. *Baby Sanders.*

The squaw recoiled and said something in Shoshone. Elizabeth said softly, "my baby." Tears were in her eyes. Her body leaned slightly forward in expectation with her hands clasped, as if in prayer. For a moment no one moved.

The squaw took off the blanket, and held it out by one corner. "Ba-by?"

"Baby." She took it gently, pressed it against her cheek and rocked from side to side. "Thank you. Thank you very much," she said softly.

"Ba-by." The squaw bobbed her head and grinned. "Ba-by."

Elizabeth slept with the blanket for the next two weeks. It was comforting for her to know that she had born a child. She was a mother. A small piece of her life had been restored.

The letter came from Fort Supply, a missionary center and supply station for Mormons heading to and from Salt Lake. A wagon train would be coming through the first week of November. Could Lewis send over some beef and potatoes?

Lewis and his boys loaded the wagon while Emily assisted Elizabeth. "That should keep your ears warm," she said as she tied the bow of the muslin pioneer bonnet under Elizabeth's chin, "and, here's a shawl. It's as thick as I could make it. Lewis put a buffalo hide in the wagon for you. It's another twelve days' ride to Salt Lake. Hopefully it doesn't snow."

"How can I ever thank you? You have been so good to me."

They hugged, parted, tearfully smiled and hugged again.

The six miles to Fort Supply went by fast, too fast for Elizabeth. She was nervous. Fort Bridger had been her refuge, her resting place, a blessing. They waited two days before the Mormons came in. The weary travelers came into the fort in droves, trading, bartering, excited to be at their last stop on a long journey westward.

"Well, I'll be…!" Lewis exclaimed. "If it isn't John Casings! I was thinking about you and Otis the other day. How are you? And your family?"

"As good as can be expected on a cold day in this windy territory. My brother and his family are in the wagon behind us.

He's around here somewhere. And you, I heard you were in Fort Bridger."

"Yes, my sons and I brought some supplies over, and I'm looking to place a passenger with someone." He put Elizabeth's hand on his arm. "This is Elizabeth Fox. She's been ill but is ready to travel now. Needs a ride to the valley. I have her food rations with me."

Brother Casings extended his hand. "I think we can manage that. My Anna will appreciate having some female companionship. I'm not much of a talker and she, well she never stops."

It was settled, the wagon was loaded and Elizabeth had her ride to Salt Lake.

Chapter Fifteen

Love Waits

Love Waits (12) followed by Reunion (13) followed by Amen (14)

The wind was from the north, bitter cold and cutting on the November day of departure. The trees were barren, angular designs of white reaching upwards. Spruce and pines had prickly green fingers peeking from layers of frozen snow and ice. The sun glazed in the cloudless, blue sky and travelers squinted to protect their eyes from the glare.

The windy territory had its blessings, the trail was clear and their feet stayed dry as they walked on the hard crust blown free of snow. The shallow creeks were iced over so the wagons easily slid across. They needed to get to the valley before a heavy snow-fall. The noon meal stop was cut to one hour and they pushed hard to cover seventeen miles per day. They were running out of time.

Anna was a cheerful soul. She delighted in everything she saw—the doe standing in the shadows of the juniper tree, the ice crystals on the rocks, the snuggle times when she would get under the blankets, hold them up like a tent inside the wagon, and tell funny stories to her children, Robert and Susannah. She had a fanciful imagination. She reminded Elizabeth of someone.

John sat on the wagon seat while the women and children stayed in the wagon bed covered with blankets. He flicked the reigns and his horses picked up the pace.

"John," Anna addressed her husband loudly and matter-of-factly. "When we get to Salt Lake we need to go directly to Aunt Mary's." Elizabeth looked incredulously at Anna.

John didn't acknowledge his wife's statement so she said it again, "John, dear. Aunt Mary's!" This time she shouted. "We need to go directly to Aunt Mary's." She emphasized 'Aunt Mary's'."

Images flashed through Elizabeth's mind. She could see herself sitting in a rocking chair. A young woman was kneeling with her head lying on her lap. And there were two others, a tall blue eyed, freckle faced boy standing with his big hand on her shoulder, and a smaller girl, with a cute turned up nose, smiling, picking the petals from a white daisy and watching them float to the ground.

Mary...I have a daughter...Mary. Eyes still closed, she watched the scene. She reached up and touched the boy's hand. "I love you, Mum," she could hear him plainly. "I love you too, Thomas."

Thomas...that's it! I have a son named Thomas. She could see herself dancing with him, stepping on his toes, laughing. *Oh, my heavens. I have two children. Mary and Thomas.*

The wagon wheels creaked, providing a background of noise that one normally chose to ignore, but now, for Elizabeth, the creaking penetrated. Eyes still closed, she could see herself riding in a wagon. A young girl ran along beside. "Come sit up here with me," she invited.

"Oh, no," she replied. "It's too bumpy." She laughed as she watched her daughter skip off to unknown discoveries. *Desdemona..., my delightful child.*

Elizabeth opened her eyes, tears frozen on her cheeks. Now she knew she had three children. She was going to her family!

The journey was arduous through the Wasatch Mountains in the beginning of winter. At night the horses pawed the snow and found nibbles of grass. Lack of good grazing and over work made them move slower, only pulling fourteen miles the last day through Golden Pass.

They camped in a clearing. The night sky was lit by a full golden moon; the kind only seen in autumn.

Elizabeth slept little. *George, I am so sorry.* Her sleepy thoughts wandered. *It must have been so hard for you. I can't imagine what I would do if I lost you. Are you all right? I can't wait to see you.* She dozed. *How will I find you? I remember. I have to find Charlotte's house. Is she helping you, George? I hope she's helping you.*

She opened her eyes in the blackness. John snored in long, slow noisy breaths. Anna turned over and sighed. A horse snorted. The sounds seemed louder at night. *How are the children?* She worried. She rubbed her arms, not from being cold, but rather from anxiety. *Are they well? Are they saying their prayers? Is someone tucking Desdemona in at night? Who's caring for*

Thomas? Is Mary in school? She's such a good reader. She shivered and scrunched further down under her buffalo hide. *(Love Waits–12)*

George, I have something to tell you. My hair is only to my shoulders now. She remembered how he would sit quietly in the evenings watching her brush her waist-length silky hair. Then he would kiss her face and neck as he ran his fingers through it. She took a deep breath. *We had to cut it. I'm sorry.* She fell asleep apologizing and woke up before dawn with a startling thought. *What if George has another wife!* She felt panic rise in her throat as she recalled Brother Matheson whose wife had died a few days before sailing from Liverpool. He married again before docking in New York, not even two months later. *No, George wouldn't do that. He couldn't do that! He's waiting for me.* Her doubts subsided with the morning light as so often is the case.

The sun melted the snow on the roads into Salt Lake leaving them rutted and muddy. From the foothills, the valley, blanketed with new fallen snow, looked like a black and white patchwork quilt with an extra large square in the middle where temple construction had begun. Coming into the city they were met by four brethren on horseback.

"Welcome." The horse reared as its rider shouted above the noise. "Do you have a place to stay?"

"Yes, we do, but we have a passenger who needs to find her family. Is there somewhere we can go to find out where the Franklin Richards' home is?"

"The council house, four blocks down. It's on the main road—big two story building on the northeast corner. Ask for Brother Whetstone. He knows where everyone lives."

"Will you tell my brother in the next wagon to follow us?"

"Sure will. God be with you." He waved them on.

They rode slowly through the wide city streets taking in all the sights. A few people had gathered to welcome their relatives and loved ones. Most were at the social. The council house was easy to find. The women held the reigns while the men went in to inquire.

Elizabeth sat on the wagon perch, face taut, back straight, hands folded in her lap. Her heart was pounding. *What if we can't find them? I don't think I've ever been so nervous.* She bit her lip.

"Relax, Lizzy." It was as if Anna read her thoughts. "We'll have you back with your family presently. Think of all those kisses and hugs you're going to get." They laughed and Elizabeth felt better.

"We're looking for Brother Whetstone." John was the spokesman.

"That would be me," the bent silver-haired man said in a high, businesslike tone. "How can I help you?"

"We have a passenger with us who needs to find her family."

"And her name would be?"

"Elizabeth Fox."

"What did you say?"

"Her name is Elizabeth Fox. We're looking for George Fox who is staying in the Franklin Richards' home."

"So he is. You are absolutely right! But you probably won't find him there tonight." He wagged his head. "I saw him today and he said he was taking his children to the social tonight in the basement of the Social Hall."

"Can you give me directions?" John spoke rapidly. He always did that when he was excited.

"As a matter of fact, I am going there myself." He shuffled his papers into a tidy stack and placed them exactly in the middle of his desk. "I'll get my coat." He grasped his cane propped against the desk and leaned heavily on it as he tottered to the wooden coat rack. "We can go over together if you would like." He thrust his hand through the sleeve of his black waistcoat, wiggled his fingers then slowly repeated the process. Finally, getting it almost to his shoulders, he shrugged quickly and it fell into its accustomed place. He grabbed his top hat and popped it on his head. He took out his pocket watch and meticulously studied it. "Yes. I do believe I can go to the social now."

"Thank you sir," John replied.

"You can ride with us," Otis added.

"I shan't be riding. Oh, no, no, no." He shook his head. "I will walk. I walk every evening. Good for the body, you know, to walk. It is exactly three blocks east and two blocks north of here. You will see it. You may bring your families in here to ready yourselves if you would like. Here is the key. Please lock the building before you leave. You can return the key to me at the social. I shall go find Brother Fox for you."

John and Otis looked at each other, then to Brother Whetstone. "Thank you very much. We will do just that, won't take us long." John's words ran together. "We'll hurry right over." They rushed out of the building.

"Did you find him?" Anna called from across the street.

"Yes, he's at a dance down the street a piece."

The families were quick to ready themselves. Anna smoothed her daughter's dress with her hands and braided her strawberry blonde hair. Otis's two teenage boys, who were taller than he, spit in their hands and rubbed their hair into place. Nothing they did made a difference in how they looked but they felt better.

"Here, for you." Anna placed a lovely lace shawl on Elizabeth's shoulders.

"Oh," she gasped, "you should wear it. It's beautiful, Anna." She ran her fingers over the ivory threads tatted into intricate patterns with delicate fringe along the edges. "It's so pretty!" Her eyes shone.

"It's a wedding gift of sorts. Happy reunion." *(Reunion–13)*

Elizabeth threw her arms around Anna and whispered, "Thank you, forever. Thank you."

"You are very welcome, Elizabeth." She hugged her dear friend and said, "Now, my dear, let's go find your husband!"

George didn't notice the stir of activity in the far corner of the Social Hall. He only heard echoes of Elizabeth's name resounding against the cliffs along the Green River. He rehearsed the frantic searching over and over in his mind.

"Can you tell me where Brother George Fox would be?" Brother Whetstone leaned forward on his cane so he could be sure to hear the reply. His intense blue eyes locked on the young woman's face.

"Over there." She pointed across the room. He hobbled slowly, dodging the dancers as he went. "Ah, there he is," he said under his breath. He recognized George from the back for many times he had watched this strong man leave his office with sagging shoulders.

"Brother Fox." He tapped him on the shoulder. "Brother Fox." Surprised to hear the clerk's familiar voice, George turned, his body tense, bracing himself for the news.

"It's about your wife," he started. George strained to hear above the music.

"My wife! Is she…?" His face was ashen. George couldn't believe it.

"Oh my, no." The clerk could tell by the fear in George's eyes that he misunderstood the purpose of his visit.

"She's not…, she's here, your wife is here." The clerk smiled broadly. It wasn't often he got to be the bearer of good news.

"She's here, where?" George's voice carried through the hall. His thoughts raced. *I knew she was alive. I knew it. Heavenly Father, thank you. Thank you.*

"Over there! Near the door." The clerk pointed with his cane.

Charlotte, standing nearby, figured out what was happening and quickly awakened Desdemona then looked for Mary and Thomas. Clusters of saints tugged at each other's elbows and whispers of the miracle filtered about the room.

The music faded, one violin at a time. The dancers moved aside as the tight group of men, still wearing their buckskins and smelling of campfires, entered the room.

John, Otis and his two sons accompanied Elizabeth. John gave her a pat on the shoulder and a nudge when he saw Brother Whetstone.

Elizabeth stood alone in the middle of the room unaware of everyone around her. Her hair was in a neat bun except for a few wispy curls that framed her face. Her skin was smooth, her eyes, shaded with long black lashes, gazed clearly. Her lips were slightly parted, in demure expectation. The rust colored dress, mended with hashed stitches in disjointed patterns, contrasted with the delicate lace shawl that gracefully hung from her shoulders.

All eyes were on George as he walked toward her and, for a brief moment, he hesitated, as if he couldn't believe his eyes. His soft whisper penetrated the silence. *(Amen–14)*

"Betsy."

He swooped her into his arms, lifting her off the floor and kissed her hair, her forehead, her cheeks, her lips. "Betsy," he whispered again and again. His face was wet with tears. Their embrace was broken by a child's voice from across the hall.

"Mum! Mum!" Desdemona ran to her mother's outstretched arms. Elizabeth scooped her up, rocked her from side to side and smothered her with kisses.

Thomas rushed up behind and nearly knocked her over when he threw his arms around her waist. She hugged him, tousled his hair, and kissed the top of his head. Then, she saw Mary. George took Desdemona into his arms and Thomas stood next to his Father as they watched.

"Mary, my dear Mary," she said tenderly. She took her daughter's hands in hers and gazed in her eyes. Then, Elizabeth pulled her close and Mary sobbed in her mother's arms.

"Mum, I thought…"

"I know, Mary, I know," she whispered.

Desdemona wriggled down from her Father's arms and took Mary's hand.

"Don't cry Mary, this is a happy time." Her innocence lightened the moment.

Mary wiped her eyes and laughed, "you're right."

Muffled laughs and sniffs were heard as George and Elizabeth embraced once again and hugged their children. They held their most precious treasures. Surely the angels of heaven must have been delighted as they viewed that small family circle together once again. Reunited. In faith. In love. In Zion.

Epilogue

Elizabeth Fox (1823-1901) continued in faith and service to her family, the church and the community. She became a midwife and delivered many babies in the Salt Lake area. Shortly after arriving in Salt Lake, the Fox family moved to Murray where George herded cattle for the Church. During the summers they took the cattle east, into the hills and the family lived in a wagon box. One summer, a man asked Elizabeth to come to his home and help his wife give birth. Before they left for Salt Lake, George gave their children instructions to listen for Indians who often tried to steal the cattle. Their parents left, the dog barked and they could hear the Indians. One child stood on each end of the wagon box and the other child loaded the guns. Every time the Indians came close they would shoot at them.

Finally the Indians left. George was very proud of his children. Desdemona was reputed to be an extremely good shot.

Elizabeth's health was generally good, however, at one time she became very ill from eating bran bread and her life was saved when Franklin D. Richards gave George some white flour for her. When he brought the flour home, a neighbor came over and said his wife was sick with the same thing and George gave him half of the flour.

While living in the wagon box in 1856, her son David was born. Another son, Heber John was born November 22, 1859. They moved to Millcreek from 1859-1864 where Elizabeth had two more children, Sarah Jane in 1861 and Franklin Richard in 1864. Both died in infancy.

It took three weeks for the family to move via wagon to Lewisville, Idaho in 1885. George and Elizabeth, their married children and grandchildren were some of the earliest settlers of Lewisville. She continued to be a midwife, even delivering some of her own grandchildren. She often used a rowboat to cross the Snake River to deliver babies or take care of the sick. When asked if she was afraid of the river (Most people knew she couldn't swim.) she would answer, "I am not afraid of the river. Someone must go and it may as well be me." She had great faith that God would take care of her.

One night, in the dead of winter, a man came to their house wanting Elizabeth, now in her 70's, to care for his wife who was about to give birth. George told him no because Elizabeth was very ill. She heard them talking and offered to go if they could wrap her in a bed in the sleigh and go across the frozen river. She said it was more important to save two lives than to save hers. She helped with the delivery and returned home to her sick bed. She always said she never suffered any ill effects from that trip.[14]

Elizabeth was a talented quilter. Her designs were creative and intricate. One of her handiworks, the tulip quilt, is referred to in the text of the book.

Authors Note: I am grateful that Elizabeth was so skilled and creative in her quilting for it was in the book "Quilts and Women of the Mormon Migrations" that I first read her story and was so touched by it.

Elizabeth died at the age of 78 on April 23, 1901. She is buried in Lewisville, Idaho. George died at the age of 85 in December 1904.

Notes

1 The ship's steward let Elizabeth keep the bowl. It is currently in the possession of Faye Burrows, the great granddaughter of Desdemona Fox.

2 The *Julia Ann* shipwrecked in 1855 just off the coast of Australia. *Saints on the High Seas*, p 58.

3 Story of blessing and angels: *Blessing and Angels: from the Life Sketches of George Sellman Fox and Mary Elizabeth Jones.*

4 Elizabeth was a creative quilter. Her skills were displayed in her "Tulip" quilt. A photograph is included in *Quilts and Women of the Mormon Migrations, Treasures of Transition.*

5 The skill of "Geeing" and "Hawing" was of utmost importance as an unruly team of oxen could tip over the wagon and cause serious accident and, even loss of life, or hold up the wagon train for repairs. *Route From Liverpool to Great Salt Lake Valley* pp 97-107.

6 The Andrus train was the last to leave Atchison Kansas on August 5, 1855. They arrived in Salt Lake on October 25. *An Enduring Legacy*, pp 367 and 368.

7 William Clayton's guide was used by every Mormon wagon train and by many others. It not only gave the topography but suggested places to stop for water, good feeding areas for the

stock as well as distances from landmarks. *Saints Find the Place, A Day by Day Pioneer Experience*, p 132.

8 The sculpture I saw in 1978 is paralleled in the book and in the performance of *Pioneer Legacy Pageant* a production based on Elizabeth Jones Fox' story and presented annually on July 23 and 24 in Springville, Utah.

9 Independence Rock was named by a group of immigrants that camped and celebrated Independence Day there. The name stuck and the tradition of etching names carried on for decades. The call for emigration in the letter of December 23, 1847 is also included in *Route From Liverpool to Great Salt Lake Valley*, p 122.

10 Bridger's place is on the Black's Fork, a tributary entering the Green River from the west. Fort Bridger had a high picket fence that enclosed a large yard for animals' protection from wild beasts and Indians. Major A. James Bridger, one of the oldest mountain men in the area, was an Indian trader for 30 years. During the Walker War in 1853 Bridger sold guns to the Indians. To protect the saints en route and secure control of the trading post, the LDS Church bought Fort Bridger from James Bridger and Louis Vasquez in 1853 for $8,000.

11 In 1855 a ward was nine blocks square with a schoolhouse in the central block. It was also used for religious meetings. Inhabitants were required to send their children when at the proper age. Everyone had to pay or the ward would pay for them. The schoolmaster was paid $50 per month. Most children attended during the winter, November-February.

12 After 8 years of plenty, in 1855 there were severe challenges in growing crops. Potatoes were infested with a black bug. Famine was imminent. The Saints had stored 7,000 bushels of wheat and by the end of the drought the reserve was down to 125 bushels. 1855-56 was one of hardest winters. Livestock died due to the hard winter.

13 Lansford W. Hastings wrote *California and Oregon*, published in 1846 to show the Echo cut off and the Weber canyon road to the south end of GSL. It was partially cut out by the Donner Party who suffered in the process. It was later cut out by the Mormons in a more practical, wagon-worthy way. Pp 54-101.

14 Family History compiled by Edith Haddon Littleford was source for epilogue. Elizabeth was a woman of great faith.

Bibliography

Bartholomew, Rebecca and Arrington, Leonard, J. *Rescue of the 1856 Handcart Companies*, Provo, Utah, Brigham Young University, 1992.

B. H. Roberts, A Comprehensive History of the Church, Century One, Vol. III, Published by the Church of Jesus Christ of Latter-day Saints, Brigham Young University Press, Provo, Utah, 1965. Campbell, Eugene E., Establishing Zion, Salt Lake City, Signature Books, 1988

Crockett, David R., *Saints Find the Place: A Day by Day Pioneer Experience,* LDS-Gems Pioneer Trek Series, Vol 3, Tucson, Arizona, LDS-Gems Press, Tucson, 1997

Cross, Mary Bywater, *Quilts and Women of the Mormon Migrations: Treasures of Transition*, Rutledge Hill Press, 1996

Family History compiled by Edith Haddon Littleford

Fife, Austin and Alta, *Saints of Sage and Saddle,* Salt Lake City, Utah, University of Utah Press, 1980

Glazier, Stewart E., and Clark, Robert S. Journal of the Trail, Salt Lake City. 1997.

Gowans, Fred R., *Fort Bridger*, Provo, Utah, Brigham Young University Press, 1975

Hal Knight and Dr Stanley B. Kimball, 111 Days to Zion, Salt Lake City, Utah, Big Moon Traders, 1997

Hastings, Lansford W., *California and Oregon*, published in 1846

Holzapfel, Richard Neitzel, *Their Faces Toward Zion, Salt* Lake City, Utah, Bookcraft, 1996

Madsen, Brigham D., ed, *A Forty-Niner in Utah: Letters and Journal of John Hudson*, Salt Lake City, Utah, Tanner Trust Fund, University of Utah Library, 1981

Madsen, Susan Arrington and Woods, Fred E., *I Sailed To Zion*, Salt Lake City, Utah, Deseret Book Co. 2000

Mormon Immigration Index-Voyages, © 2000 by Intellectual Reserve, Inc. journal of Elder Peter Reid, a passenger on *The Samuel Curling* in 1855. compiled by Edith Haddon Littleford.

Neff, Andrew Love, *History of Utah, 1847-1869* Salt Lake City, Utah Deseret News Press, 1940

Paxman, Shirley B., *Homespun*, Salt Lake City, Utah, Deseret Book Co., 1976

Piercy, Frederick, *Route From Liverpool to Great Salt Lake Valley*, edited by Fawn M. Brodie, Cambridge, Massachusetts, The Belknap Press of Harvard University Press, 1962

Schindler, Harold, *Crossing the Plains*, Salt Lake City, Utah, Tribune, Salt Lake City 1997

Sonne, Conway B., *Saints on the High Seas*, Salt Lake City, University of Utah Press, 1983.

Stegner, Wallace, *The Story of the Mormon Trail*, New York, USA, McGraw-Hill Book Company, 1964

West from Fort Bridger: The Pioneering of Immigrant Trails Across Utah, 1846-1850. Edited by J. Roderic Korus and Dale L. Morgan, Revised and Updated by Will Bagley and Harold Schindler. Logan, Utah State University Press, 1994

About the Author

Lynne Thompson was born in 1946 in San Antonio, Texas. She was raised in Montana and Washington. She received her ballet training from the Ivan Novikoff School of Russian Ballet, Cornish School of Fine Arts in Seattle and the University of Washington.

She started teaching ballet in 1966. She currently teaches at Brigham Young University and is owner/director of the Academy of Ballet.

Through her ballet school, she has directed over 35 major ballet productions involving hundreds of dancers. She has also produced the stage productions of *Promised Valley (1978)* and *Sound of Music (1979)* and choreographed *1776 (1976)* and *Brigadoon (1980)*.

Lynne has had a lifelong interest in pioneers and the American West. In 1976 She wrote the first scenario for her pioneer ballet. In 1996, after months of research she set the scenario around Elizabeth Jones Fox' story. In 1997 she directed the original production of that scenario: the ballet, *Living Waters* and it was performed for the BYU Women's Conference at Brigham Young University in 1998.

Committed to sharing Elizabeth's story with as many people as possible, she and her husband modified the ballet into a pageant, adding lyrics to the music, narration, and drama to the choreography. Performed in an outdoor setting, the Pioneer Legacy Pageant has an enormous following with over 2000 people attending each year. Admission is free.

Since 1999 she and her husband, David, have spent their summers directing Pioneer Legacy Pageant every July 23rd and 24th.

Together, David and Lynne have raised thirteen children and have twenty grandchildren. They reside in Orem, Utah.